ZODIAC LOVERS

Paranormal Romance

Book Four

SCORPIO ✶ SAGITTARIUS ✶ CAPRICORN

LANCE TAUBOLD

DEDICATION

FOR DON AND HELENE AND ALL OUR "PARANORMAL"
EXPERIENCES.

BUT MOSTLY FOR OUR PARANORMAL FRIENDSHIP …
WITH LOVE.

TABLE OF CONTENTS

SCORPIO

The Scorpion

Traits: Emotional, Intuitive, Passionate, Magnetic, Exciting, Powerful, Determined, Jealous, Resentful, Secretive, Obstinate, Compulsive, Obsessive, Need great self-discipline, Strong reasoning powers, Self-confident, Shrewd, Propensity for outspokenness with little regard for the consequences.

"No tea leaves. No readings. I promise. Pleeez," the corpulent young man begged as he toyed with the hair on a particularly ugly voodoo doll. He set the doll back on the store's shelf and lightly stamped his foot. "Rainey, for meee. I'll be your best friend."

"You are my best friend, Ed. And don't call me Rainey. Especially with that whiney voice," Rainier Cantrell said, brushing his sun-bleached locks from his forehead. "This store is doing fine without me. It's on a well-trafficked street. It's big, but not too big. You can see all the displays. It's tastefully decorated—basically—not too gay, and you've got that nice little private—ish corner over there for readings. Of course, if you got rid of those heinous voodoo dolls that you seem to be obsessed with, things might get better. But that doesn't mean I would come back. Besides, you know what happened the last time I did a reading for your customer. He tried to sue you and me."

"Well, you didn't have to tell him he was going to get hit by a car. I mean, who says things like that? And I'm not getting rid of my dolls. People want to hear nice things, Rainey, especially from a gay psychic. You know... you're going to meet a tall, dark stranger and have the most mind-blowing sex ever."

"I did tell him that."

2

"Yes, you did. And it turned out to be that incredibly hunky doctor who took care of him. Which is why he dropped the case." Ed had was now peering at his freshly manicured nails. "Do you think I should paint my nails?" His southern drawl now came on strong.

"No, Miss Scarlett. And you may be a queen, but you don't have to advertise it. Not that there's any doubt," he added. "Now, are you going to go pick up little Eddy or not. I'm sure he misses you." Rain meandered through the various tables and displays, trying to get Ed to follow him to the front door and get this over with. "What was wrong with him anyway?

"Nothing. He's just having his teeth cleaned, but I think they put him under to do it."

"Good idea. He'd probably bite?"

"Do you bite when you're having your teeth cleaned?"

"No. But I'm not a ten-pound Yorkie with an attitude." Rain reached for the door handle.

"Nine-point-six. And you're just mad because he bit your toe last time you were here. It was your own fault. You should have picked him up. He just does it for attention. How can you resist that cute little face?" he said and pinched Rain's cheeks as he said it.

"I didn't say he wasn't cute." He pushed Ed's hands away. "But do I have to pet him all the time?"

"He needs love, just like you do. You should appreciate it, since you can't find any of your own."

"That was a low blow."

3

"But so true. Only your best friend will really tell you the truth, however painful," Ed said, then turned and walked back to a nearby table and bent over to look in a small ornate mirror. "Do I look all right?" He slowly turned his three-hundred-pound bulk in a circle.

"My turn to be honest?" Rain said with a smirk.

"Oh, you're just so mean and vindictive. And I shouldn't be more than an hour or so."

"An hour?"

"Well, I have to stop at Exotica Petica and get my baby some treats. It's traumatic, you know."

"More like dramatic. And he doesn't need any treats. He's fat enough."

"He is not fat. Just healthy."

"Like his mommy."

"Right. Have fun. Thanks, ever so." He waved and sailed out the door.

An hour. Now what? He walked around the store checking out the multiple displays. Ed had obviously worked very hard on them. Not his taste, but well displayed anyway.

When Rain first came to Atlanta from Pittsburgh, he lived with Ed and worked for him in the shop here on Piedmont Avenue, not too far from Ed's Ansley Park home. It was a good location and lot of gays lived and worked there. Both living arrangements and job had worked out fine for a while. Then he could sense Ed's jealousy every time he brought home a new, potential boyfriend—not that there had been many—and they certainly hadn't lasted long (Two months was his best.)—but still. Ed wasn't exactly dripping with boyfriends. He was a great friend and a fun-loving guy. It was just, well, he did weigh three-hundred pounds—give or take. Not every guy's fantasy. Ed did realize that that was the reason for his dearth of dates, but he had his "Little Eddy" and his shop, and he seemed perfectly contented for now. Good for him. Rain wished he could feel so contented. As for working in the shop, "Sexy Psychics," it was fun at first. Then there were the crazies and the compulsives, all wanting a fantastic future with the man—or occasionally woman—of their dreams. People sensed he was the real deal and believed what they were told. He tried to lighten the unpromising futures he saw for some of them in his tea-leaf readings, but they would start to sense when he wasn't being totally forthcoming. So, he had begun to think of looking for other work.

He'd found it, through somewhat odd circumstances, right down the street. He was the manager/partner now of a very nice men's clothing store. The clothes were different and trendy, and people listened to his suggestions and usually bought from him. The owner, an older gay man, Gene, had been so pleased with him that he'd offered to make him a partner with an option to buy him out in the future. Gene had plans with his husband of thirty years to retire to Costa Rica. Rain had taken him up on his offer, and with a loan from Ed, had become a partner.

Which was why he would do the occasional requested reading or watch the store for Ed when he needed him to. Like now. He felt slightly obligated and had paid back most of the money he'd borrowed, but they were best friends and the other parade of psychics Ed had hired for the store never seemed to stay long. Most of them thought it was an exotic and intriguing idea and would tell Ed they were really psychic and could tell wonderful futures, but none, so far, had panned out. The most current one was into recommending what club the customers should go to on what night to find the man of their dreams. Just trash.

Ed had periodically begged him to come back, but he explained that he was invested in the store and he couldn't just give it up. The actual truth, and more to the point, was that he had gotten too discouraged seeing the bleak futures for so many of the people he read for. It had become disheartening. He refused to lie, out-rightly anyway. And glossing over the truth was just not his thing either, in spite of Ed's whining, "Rainey, you don't have to tell them the bad parts, only the good." This oft-said phrase brought to mind the incident just prior to the one that had changed his life.

* * *

"Why do you need me here? Anyone can make up shit," he'd told Ed after a particularly disgruntled man wanted to know if his boyfriend had been cheating on him. Rain had really liked the guy and didn't want to see him get hurt anymore, and so had told him the truth. The guy had thrown a fit and broke several crystal figurines and knocked over a display case, yelling, "He is not cheating. He loves me. You're a liar!"

"That's it, Ed. I can't do this anymore. People are crazy. What good is it having this gift—if that's what you want to call it—if I can't do any good with it?" he had told Ed after the fiasco.

Ed had tried to placate him. "I know, sweetie. But sometimes you tell them good things."

"I just don't think I can do this anymore."

Then, the next night, Gene had come in and asked for a reading. They hit off right away.

"I've heard a lot about you young man and thought I would check you out," Gene said by means of an introduction. "Four sugars, please." He indicated the tea cup sitting in front of him. "Eugene Menendez. Call me Gene." He extended his hand.

"Thank you, I think. I hope some of it was good." He shook the man's hand. "Rainier Cantrell. Call me Rain." He poured the tea and plopped in the requested sugar cubes.

"Well, Rainer-Cantrell-call-me-Rain, the good-looking part certainly was true." The older man flirted with Southern charm, sat, and began sipping his tea.

"Thank you. What else have you heard?" Wariness came over him.

"Just that you gave tea-leaf readings that were pretty accurate but could sometimes be scary."

Scary was a new word. "Scary?"

7

"Well, just that some gentlemen were afraid to come back because you'd been dead-right with your predictions." He tapped Rain on the nose. "Which is why I'm here. I'm thinkin' of makin' some changes and am at a crossroads as to what to do. And I thought, what the heck, let's give that cute psychic boy I've heard so much about a try. It can't hurt." He paused. "Can it?"

Rain sensed the man's playful banter belied his tone. The man was here for better or worse. "I try not to hurt anyone's feelings, but it's hard for me to be dishonest. I see things and I want to help, but it doesn't always work out that way." He pulled himself upright.

"Somethin' wrong?" Gene said.

"No. It's just that I've never told anyone that before, a customer that is."

"My boy, I like you, other than your good looks. I think we're gonna get along just fine. Now, tell me what you see." He proffered the tea cup. "And don't hold back. I'm Southern. I can handle anythin'." He smiled and tapped Rain on the nose again.

Rain studied the leaves and looked with puzzlement and surprise.

"What is it, boy? I can handle it." The man became serious.

"It's... nothing bad. It's... kind of awkward though."

"Spill it, boy."

"You're going to take on a new person in your business, a clothing store isn't it?"

"Yes. Very good start, boy. I'm just down the street. "Riches To Riches, and I'm always taking on new person," he said with a touch of rue in his voice

"I've been in there quite a few times. I've never seen you. It's always some very good-looking, model-type in there."

"Yes, there have been quite a few. Can't get good help nowadays. Especially, the cute ones. But I like having them in there. It brings the boys in. Nobody wants to come in and see an old man like me. So, I stay in the back." He put a hand to his chest.

"Well, I think you're very dashing," Rain said, and meant it.

"Flattery will get you everywhere." He turned the three-syllable word into six and gave another nose tap. "And I'm sixty-one, but you probably knew that. Now, who is this gorgeous new hunk who is goin' to come work for me?"

"Me," Rain said with a self-deprecating smirk.

Gene let out a loud, "Ha," and laughed. "Well, if this isn't the strangest way to get a job I've ever heard."

"Actually, the strangest part, is that I seldom see myself in any of my readings, unless, of course, it's some boyfriend of mine who insists on a reading. But that's a whole other drama," Rain said with disgust.

"Do tell. Since, apparently, you're goin' to be workin' for me. I do like to know some background about my employees."

Rain found himself wanting to tell the man, and so he did. "My love life sucks, to put it bluntly."

"I find that hard to believe, with your dashin' good looks and that nicely toned body of yours."

"That's because I have no love life. I can spend a lot of time in the gym." He took a deep breath. "Here goes. Every time I get a prospective boyfriend and they find out what I do, they either scoff at me and leave or, even worse, want me to give them a reading."

"Uh oh. Honesty isn't always the best policy, I'm thinkin'," Gene interjected.

"Right. I use every excuse I can to avoid it. But then they'll get mad or say that I'm a fake... and ultimately, I give in, hoping that maybe I'll see a future with them. But no. I always see the end of the relationship. Oh, I don't always tell them that's what I see. Sometimes, I'll hope against hope that I'm wrong, or that I can change the future, but it inevitably ends the same. Sometimes sooner, sometimes later. Maybe I sabotage myself and subconsciously know it's doomed and so I don't try. But I don't think so."

"Are you ever wrong?"

Rain just looked at him.

"That look just spoke volumes." Gene fanned himself. "So, do we have a future together?"

"As far as I can see." Rain now tapped Gene on the nose.

Gene laughed heartily. "I'm very glad, my boy. Very glad. But let me ask you somethin'. Why don't you just look into your own tea leaves and find your Mr. Right?"

"There's the ironic part. I can't read my own leaves. It's just a bunch of muddied leaves in a cup. I wish I could. Life would be so much easier."

"Maybe, it's not supposed be, Rain," he said, thoughtfully. "Perhaps, God has somethin' or someone special in mind for you."

"Perhaps. But I wish he'd hurry. I'm thirty-three and this gym body and good looks aren't going to last forever," he said, again self-deprecatingly.

"Well, you are a good-lookin' boy. Inside and out. Don't you doubt it." Two nose taps this time. "So, when do you want to start workin' for me?"

* * *

That had been a year-and-a-half ago. Ed understood, but, of course, played up the drama of his "desertion." And then, six months ago, Gene had offered the partnership. There had been no more readings for Gene. He was satisfied and so was his partner of thirty years, Ralph, another good-old southern gentleman.

Rain began to rearrange the shelf of hideous voodoo-type dolls so that the obvious painstaking workmanship of the dolls was better displayed. They were very artistic. Maybe he'd get one for Gene as a joke. They were ugly but... His birthday was coming up soon and he was born on Halloween. It seemed appropriate. Gene would get a kick out of it, especially coming from him. Gene still liked to hear all about any of his readings or predictions whenever he filled in at Ed's store. Ed would still get the frequent call from someone who wanted a reading, and since Ed had been so kind as to let him borrow the money for the partnership, he would, reluctantly, do it.

The bells on the front door clanged.

Rain looked up from the display and dropped the doll he had been holding on the floor. "Oh my God!" he said before he could stop himself.

Rain looked into the dark blue eyes of the most beautiful man he'd ever seen. His black hair and olive skin perfectly set off the hue of his mesmerizing eyes. Rain felt the connection like a bolt of lightning.

"Excuse me?" uttered the rich baritone, the gaze intent— slight smile and a nod of the head. "I hope I didn't frighten you."

Rain could hear the Southern in the man's voice now. He didn't have a response. Well, he did, but it wouldn't have been too appropriate. So he said, "No," and felt his voice break a little.

The man approached him. "Creighton Marlin."

The man, who was a good three or four inches taller than Rain, leaned down into Rain. He thought the man was going to kiss him and found himself closing his eyes in anticipation. "You dropped this, I believe."

Rain's eyes snapped open. The dropped doll was before him. He felt himself blush from head to toe.

"Charming. I didn't mean to embarrass you. But it's charming all the same."

"Oh, you didn't," Rain countered, the perspiration on his brow belying his statement.

"Of course not." The man smiled, showing perfect white teeth in sharp contrast to his dark complexion.

Rain felt himself start to blush again. He quickly grabbed the doll and turned away, placing it on the shelf, desperately hoping the man couldn't see his face reddening. "Ed, the owner, should be back in about an hour. I'm just filling in, but if there's something I could help you with?"

"I'm certain there is," the dark voice whispered just behind him. Southern had never sounded so sexy. Rain could feel the warm breath on the back of his neck. He couldn't turn around because he knew he would be right up against the man. He started to play with some of the dolls higher up on the shelves and inevitably knocked one off.

"Allow me." The man reached down and brushed Rain's back, retrieved the doll, and placed it back on the upper shelf. Rain inhaled a slight waft of citrus mixed with a musky smell as the man's arm was raised next to his face—not at all unpleasant.

"Pardon me." The man inclined his head down toward Rain, arm still raised.

Rain looked up, sure he was going to be kissed this time.

He wasn't disappointed.

The man's arm came down and pulled his head to his own. The rich full lips covered Rain's and the kiss deepened. Mouths opened, tongues connected. Rain's arms slid up the man's quite muscular back and pulled him close. The man's arousal was apparent, as Rain was sure his own was also.

Their lips slowly parted.

"I wish I could honestly say I was sorry. But I'd be lyin'. And I never lie." His face was mere inches from Rain's. "But I will say that I have never kissed a man after just meeting him, but I couldn't help myself. You're very powerful."

Powerful. Rain had never heard that word used before to describe him. On the other hand, this man—what did he say his name was?... Creighton?—he was powerful. And that kiss! Potent, powerful, intoxicating. And he wanted more.

"I can honestly say that I have never done that either." He paused. Should he say it? What the hell? "And I'm not sorry either."

"I'm glad." Creighton lowered his head again.

"RAINEY! We're ba-ack!"

The door's bells clanged and Ed came soaring into the store.

The two men jumped apart.

"Well, am I interrupting somethin'? Perhaps I should go out and come back in again."

And he did.

"Rainey?" Creighton smiled.

"An obnoxious nickname." Rain snarled.

"It's kind of cute." He brushed the locks on Rain's forehead.

"RAINEY! We're ba-ack!" Ed sailed in again. He approached Creighton, a delicate hand extended. I'm Ed, owner of this fine establishment, and Rainey's best friend in the whole wide world.

"Not anymore," Rain said, under his breath.

"I am in the same room, Rainey." Ed still held out his hand.

Creighton took the proffered hand, bent over, and lightly kissed it. "Charmed to meet you."

"Oh my stars! I believe I have the vapors!" Ed began to fan himself. "I might never wash this hand again."

"Ed, must you? This is Creighton..."

"Marlin," Creighton supplied.

"Right. And can your perpetual "Gone With The Wind" recitation. You have a potential customer here."

"Why of course. I know that. But do you?" Ed fanned himself again.

Rain felt himself begin to redden again. "Creighton was just helping me fix this display."

"Well, if that's how you go about fixin' a display, feel free to fix my displays anytime." Ed put a hand to his chest.

"Ed, did you just actually bat your eyes?" Rain asked, appalled.

"Of course. Now, how may I help you, you dashing rogue?"

Creighton began to laugh. "You are absolutely delightful, Ed."

"See, Rainey." He gave a condescending nod to Rain.

"Actually, I'm here for a reading. Friends of mine encouraged me to come here. They told me that there was a wonderful psychic who read tea leaves and that I needed—"

Rain made a quick intake of breath.

"Something wrong?" Creighton turned to him.

"Not at all, dear boy," Ed said. "And it seems as if providence has smiled on you. Our expert tea-leaf reader just happens to here tonight." Ed put his hand to Creighton's chest. "Oo, nice and firm. But I guess, Rainey, you'd know that." He rubbed Creighton's chest some more.

"Where is your reader?"

Ed made a slow-motion arc with his head, eyes meeting Rain's. "Right next to you."

"The plot thickens." Creighton smiled at Rain and his eyes grew intense. "Would you mind indulging me?"

The irony not lost on any of them.

Rain wanted to refuse the request, but found himself nodding anyway.

Creighton continued, "I have to tell you, however, that I don't take much stock in this. I lost a bet and promised I would come here. I do have to say, though, that I'm very glad I have. I don't mean to impugn what you do, but I have to let you know what you're up against."

Rain found himself taking umbrage at this and was just about to defend himself, when Ed—of course—cut in.

"Oh, Rainey's the best. You'll change your mind, I'm sure. This way." He took Creighton's hand and led him to the back of the store. Rain followed, silent now.

"Here, have a seat." Ed indicated the small chair at the short cocktail table set in the far back corner of the store. "I'll get the tea."

Rain sat opposite Creighton and said, "Why are you here if you're so skeptical?"

"I didn't mean to offend you. As I told you, I lost a bet. And to be honest, I've never done anything like this before, but my personal life has been—how shall I put it—less than successful, and my friends suggested this and we made this ridiculous bet while I had been drinking, and I lost. So, here I am. I do have to say, that now I'm here, I am intrigued. But please forgive my skepticism."

The double meaning was not lost on Rain, and he had to admit that he was definitely intrigued as well. That kiss had been amazing. And what the hell, what was one more impossible future for him anyway. At least he could get this over with before it started and he became disappointed again. But he knew this man was somehow different. If he got involved, this relationship would be intense, and he didn't know if he could handle the inevitable break-up. Best to not let it start.

"Here's your tea, boys." Ed disrupted Rain's thoughts. "I'll just leave you two alone. "Remember, Rainey, good things." He wafted away, but not too far.

"Good things?" Creighton said, taking a sip of the tea.

"I have a tendency to be too honest in my readings. Sometimes people aren't so pleased, which is why I only fill in here occasionally, when Ed is in dire straits."

"I can handle honesty." Creighton took another sip. "And I respect it. Would you like to have dinner after this?"

"Yes. I mean, no. I should get home." Rain couldn't believe he'd agreed so readily.

"Honesty?"

Rain was caught. "Yes. I would like to." He was now determined that this man would trust him. It seemed important that he did.

Creighton finished his tea. "I know a wonderful little place very near my home. Now, what do you see?" He pushed the cup toward Rain.

Rain peered into the fine bisque Limoges cup. Ed believed in the best. Rain went into that "other place" inside his head. He didn't understand it. He just went with it. It was like his brain opened up a hidden door and let the visions come through. He'd never described it to anyone. They would have been too creeped out.

The door opened.

He laughed softly. "I see dinner with me. I see many dinners with me. Strolling. Holding hands. A mansion. Your house. Your bedroom. A canopy bed. Gold brocade comforter. You pick me up and throw me on the bed. You slowly take off your clothes... I'm smiling. You laugh and jump on me. You're driving... a Maybach? Alone. Singing. "Come Fly With Me." There's a—"

Rain abruptly stopped. "That's it. Sorry. I've never done that."

"Stopped? Or what? What did you see?" Creighton pressed.

"No. I... I didn't see anymore. That was it." A bad lie, he knew. "This is all just awkward. It sounds so much like I want to date you. I don't. I mean, it wouldn't be right. I can't. It would never—"

"Calm down. I won't pressure you. Persuade, maybe. But that's my nature. It was a charming way to start a relationship."

"But I just told you I can't."

"The tea leaves say differently. Do they ever lie?"

"Well, no, but... I can't."

"Can't or won't? Are you afraid of me? I'm not all that scary."

"No, you're not."

Creighton laughed. "I appreciate that."

"I mean. You're not scary at all. Just the opposite. But I never set up dates this way."

"No. Never," Ed, who had been unfathomably silent this whole time, interjected as he moved to them. "He has never done this before. There might be somethin' special here, Rainey. I think he's mighty special." He put a hand to Creighton's cheek.

"Thank you, Ed, for your vote of confidence. And now I'm starving. Let's go get that dinner you envisioned. Where do we go?"

"Quarrel's. For barbecue," he paused, swallowing. "And Mint Juleps."

"Well, they do have the best of both. Shall we?"

"I shouldn't do this."

"Why ever not?" Ed almost shouted. "I know you're from the North, but I didn't think you were a total ninny hammer. And besides, he's gorgeous. And if you don't go, I will."

19

"Please." Creighton put his hand over Rain's. "Just one date." He squeezed. "Don't be a ninny hammer."

Rain burst out laughing. "You even make ninny hammer sound sexy. All right. I'll go. Just one date."

"Praise the Lord!" Ed shouted.

Rain turned away. A furrow came to his brow. The inchoate feeling of disaster he'd felt from the reading still lingered. He'd ended it before he saw too much. What had he missed? Something felt wrong. He should have continued, but a feeling had told him to stop. He needed to know what happened next. He sensed a possible future with Creighton, and knew he could fall hard for him. In spite of the dark feeling, he wanted to give it a try. Maybe this would be the man for him. He desperately wanted someone. He hated his gift. It was more of a curse and he would have gladly relinquished it. He just wanted normal. A normal relationship. A normal guy. A normal life. "Please, God, let this work out."

* * *

"Creighton's an unusual name," Rain said, then scoffed. "This coming from a guy named Rainier. And before you ask, my mom had a thing for Prince Rainier. Actually, I did, too. Which is kind of creepy, a mother and son lusting after the same guy."

Creighton began to laugh. And laugh. The other nearby customers in Quarrel's stared... and admired. After a good thirty seconds, he wiped the tears from his eyes and said, emphasizing his drawl, "Do you always try to impress this way on a first date? And Creighton is a family name."

Rain was mortified. What in the world had gotten into him? "I... I'm so sorry. I've never said anything like that before. You must think I'm the biggest kind of fool."

Creighton slid his chair around the table and next to Rain, leaned over and kissed him full on the mouth. They melded. A couple of customers audibly sighed. "I think you're delightful. I've never been so charmed or taken with any man before."

Rain was spell-struck. That kiss was his undoing, the heat from it so intense he was sure the buttons on his shirt had melted. He literally could not speak. He just stared into those intense blue eyes and revealed his soul. Vulnerable didn't begin to cover how he felt.

Open.

Raw.

Naked.

Scared.

This was the man. He knew it as sure as he ever knew anything. He couldn't tear his gaze away from Creighton's. He didn't want to.

They stared into each other, the raw emotion almost palpable.

"Lordy, that's hot!" an older man from the adjacent table gushed.

The exclamation broke their gaze.

Creighton smiled. "This is a gay restaurant after all."

The spell broken, Rain said, wryly, "It seems that we're the floor show."

They both looked around. Nearly every table was now watching them with conspicuous anticipation.

"This is better than when we saw *Wicked* over at the Alliance," the 'Lordy' man said, none too discreetly.

His dinner partner slapped him. "Shush. You're too loud— even if it is true."

Rain and Creighton heard every word. Creighton turned to the gentlemen. "Gentlemen, I sincerely hope not, as I have tickets for Saturday night. But thank you just the same."

"Ahem." The waiter, who had been hovering for the past few minutes, immensely enjoying "the show" also, finally interrupted. "Anything else?" There was an audible squeak in his voice.

Creighton turned to him and displayed his most devastating smile. "Yes. Please buy these handsome gentlemen two of your best cognacs on me." He referenced the older couple.

"I declare," the Lordy man said, "chivalry is alive and well in Atlanta. Thank you, kind sir. You've revitalized my faith in the gay human race. True love still exists." He raised an arm to them as if he were raising a standard into battle.

"Must you?" his partner said.

"Yes. I must. Drink your brandy, you old fool." The drinks had arrived as swiftly as they'd been ordered. "To love everlasting!" he toasted Rain and Creighton.

The partner said, "To love everlasting," as he looked into his partner's eyes.

They clinked snifters, stared at one another, smiled, and sipped the fiery liquid—eyes locked.

Rain, oddly silent during all of this, finally said, "I think I might cry."

"Beautiful, isn't it? That's what I want." Creighton looked intently into Rain's eyes.

Rain wanted to be embarrassed, wanted to turn away, knew he should turn away... but he didn't. He wanted that, too. "Gold brocade?" he said.

"You'll love how it feels." Creighton said, throwing some bills onto the table and taking Rain's hand as they stood.

Rain glanced back at the older men, who were too now involved in one another to notice him.

✳ ✳ ✳

Rain slid on the brocade comforter slightly as Creighton slid into him. The woven threads lightly scratched and stimulated Rain's chest and nipples, the feeling exquisite—a perfect fit, despite Rain's mild apprehension at Creighton's size.

They'd entered Creighton's bedroom, silently, the air about them heated to a fever pitch. Rain noticed not one detail of the room, his eyes riveted to the incredible man before him as Creighton's were on him. They'd gone directly to the bed. Creighton had paused, slid his arms under Rain, picked him up and tossed him on the bed, and said, "Making sure the tea leaves don't lie." Then he'd pounced on Rain and they'd begun kissing and caressing. Sometimes slowly, sometimes rushed. Their clothes had dissolved while they'd worshipped each other's bodies from head to foot and back again, neither one denying or decrying the other's wants or preferences, simply giving over to one another and noting particularly sensitive areas to return to for a more thorough treatment. The continued fondling went on and on until neither one could bear it any longer and had advanced to the next ineluctable stage.

Rain, never being particularly dominant or submissive, went with the natural flow of things—and right now nothing had ever felt more natural. The slow rhythmic movements and the nuzzling and caressing of his back and ears were all he could stand without crying out his pleasure. He felt warm, long fingers move slowly down his side, leaving a trail of fire where they touched. The hands went lower and now his flanks received the same treatment, this time with a gentle kneading.

"Ahh," he couldn't help uttering.

"Am I hurting you?" came the husky baritone in his ear.

"No, I..." Creighton's hand found its way beneath him and began kneading in a different, pulsing way this time.

"I'm impressed," came the baritone again, the voice becoming more breathless as his other hand moved up to Rain's shoulder to clasp the hand there.

Rain couldn't last much longer. The kneading and stroking became more insistent, in tune with the ever-increasing, vigorous thrusting. His head writhed as Creighton licked and gently bit his neck, his breath harsh and hot. The air in the room, thick and musky, added to the heightened sensations. His pelvis rocked in counterpoint to Creighton's movements, wanting more of him—and receiving it.

"Creighton, I'm..."

"I know, my love. Me too."

The endearment sent Rain over the top, and he felt Creighton also achieve his pleasure. "Ahhh!" The powerful expletive came simultaneously from both men.

Rain basked in the moist warmth and weight of Creighton still on top of him and holding him tightly.

"You're mine," Creighton whispered.

The breath in his ear sent tingling sensations through Rain as he felt himself relishing the words, not second-guessing, just accepting—knowing they were true.

✳ ✳ ✳

"Tea?" Creighton said, setting the cup on the breakfast nook table in front of Rain.

"Sure," Rain said, with a wry smile. "Why not? Look where it got me." He looked into the beautiful man's eyes as he said it.

Warmth and love came shooting back at him. "I'm glad you enjoyed the evening."

"What's not to enjoy? The best sex I've ever had with the most gorgeous man I've ever met?"

"The feeling is mutual." Creighton gave a slight head nod and drained his cup. "Feel like telling me what today is going to be like? Although, I doubt you'll ever be able to outdo last night's prediction."

Rain tried to stop himself from stiffening, but Creighton caught the movement. "I'm sorry. I didn't mean to offend you."

Rain sighed. "No, it's all right. I just..." Should he tell him? Somehow he knew he must in order for there to be any future for them—and he desperately wanted there to be one. He continued, "I've never told a prospective boyfriend this before, but whenever they ask me, or threaten me, or scoff at me to read their leaves, I ultimately see their futures, and up till now they always exclude me. That's why I hesitate. If I see the end of the relationship, why go further with it?" He looked intently at Creighton. "I know we've only had one night, but I feel differently about you than anyone I've ever met. If I scare you... I scare you. But I want to be upfront and honest from the beginning, if there's going to be a future."

"You don't scare me. Just the opposite. I want there to be a future too with you. Something is working here to put us together. I feel very strongly about you. Now that kind of scares me. But in a good, exciting way, as if I've finally found a direction, a purpose. A home." He took Rain's hand. "I hope I'm not scaring you now."

"No, I..."

"Tell me, my love."

That endearment again. He had to tell him.

He peered into the cup.

"Quarrel's again. You, me, Gene. Brunch. Mimosas. Gene's store. You buying clothes. A lot of them. For you and me. Gene handing me keys and papers. He's giving me his store. He kisses you. Then me. He has luggage. I think he just gave me the store. Ralph comes in—hugs us both. They leave. You pick me up. Twirl me. We kiss. Driving. Your car. Nighttime. Your arm around me. You kiss me. Bright lights." His voice became agitated. "I scream... NO!"

Blackness.

"Rain! Rain! My darling, talk to me. It's okay. I'm here."

Rain jerked awake to the comforting sounds of Creighton's voice, as he was cradled in his arms on the floor.

"You fell out of the chair and onto the floor," Creighton said. "You gave me the scare of my life. I could almost feel my hair turn gray. What happened? What did you see?"

Rain was hesitant. "We were in your car, I think."

"Was it the Maybach? I'll sell it today?"

"No, it was smaller. Do you have another car?"

Creighton did his best to look abashed. "Four."

"Four?"

"I like cars. Which one was it?"

"I don't know. It was dark—and before you say it, don't sell them all. It won't matter."

"What else did you see?" Creighton pushed.

"Nothing else." He stared into space. "Maybe an accident? I don't know. I blacked out. I've never done that before in a reading." He paused, trying to piece his vision together. "Maybe I blacked out in my vision. I don't know." He sat up, exiting Creighton's arms.

Creighton rose, extending a hand to Rain. "You need to lay yourself down for a while. I'll make us both another cup of tea. I think I've got some chamomile somewhere. That should help you relax."

"All right. But only if you join me."

"I had every intention of doin' so. I think a little therapeutic massage is in order."

The vision all but forgotten, Rain began to unbutton his shirt.

Creighton stared as Rain's shirt dropped to the floor.

Rain stared blatantly into Creighton's eyes, and with a slight smile said, "You'd better hurry up with that tea before I fall back to sleep."

Creighton groaned softly. "Would it be rude of me to lick my lips? You look delicious."

"How about you lick my lips instead?" He approached Creighton, lips parted, and branded him with his mouth.

A half hour later, Rain once again lay cradled in Creighton's arms on the breakfast nook floor. The only difference this time was... they were naked.

"As incredible as that was, this floor is not very comfortable," Creighton said, kissing the top of Rain's head.

"I know. I'm just thinking."

"About?" the baritone voice murmured into his hair.

"My vision. I'm trying to make sense of it. It seemed like there might have been an accident, but maybe not, but I don't have good feeling about it. Maybe this is a bad idea."

"This. Is not a bad idea. Frankly, it's the best idea of my life. You are not goin' anywhere. Unless it's with me. You are mine now. As old-fashioned as that may sound. I'm not lettin' you go. Nothin' is goin' to stop this... not even you." He thumped the crown of Rain's head for emphasis. "We have something special here. You know that as well as I do. We can't throw it away over some crazy vision—"

Rain stiffened.

"Oh, my love, I didn't mean that. I know what you do is real. It's just— We can beat this. You saw us together, right?"

Rain nodded.

"Then that must mean we're meant to be together. You told me you've never seen yourself lasting with any other man. This must be it. I must be the one." He pulled Rain up to face him. "I love you, Rainier Cantrell."

Rain just stared at this beautiful man and knew he felt the same.

"You managed to worm your handsome, sexy, Yankee self right into my heart. And you're not goin' to leave it. Not ever. And I am goin' to use every bit of my dashing Southern charm to make you love me too. Do you hear me?"

Rain smiled slowly. "Don't bother—"

"Did you hear what I—"

"I already love you too."

Creighton jerked back. Rain watched the moisture come into his eyes. And more. Love. He could actually see love. It wasn't something indefinable. It was staring right into his face. He knew his own reflected what he saw, and he felt his own eyes grow damp. The magnetic pull of love drew their faces together, lips parted. Then slowly, Rain joined his lips to Creighton's to seal their futures together.

Hours later, after making it back to the bedroom, Creighton, raised on one elbow, stared down at his love. Brushing back a lock from Rain's forehead, he said, "Are we having brunch with—Gene, is it?—on Saturday or Sunday? I'll have to make a reservation."

Rain grabbed Creighton's hand and kissed it. "Sunday. I have to prepare him and tell him about you."

"Of course. How could I forget? He has to know that you're happy and taken care of." He put his hand on Rain's cheek. "And that you've found the man of your dreams. Or visions, anyway."

"Yes. He'll know that if I saw your future with me in it, it's the real thing." Rain paused. "It is real, isn't it?"

"Don't you ever doubt it." Creighton squeezed Rain's hand hard. "I've waited my whole life for you. I'm not just goin' to throw it all away like some... some... ninnyhammer."

Rain smiled. "Are you going to use that word for the rest of our lives?"

"I like it. It's cute. Like you," he said, as he bent to cover Rain's mouth with his own.

✳ ✳ ✳

"Creighton Marlin! Oh my stars, boy. You've landed yourself a winner," Gene gushed.

"You know him?" Rain said.

"Not personally. But I've seen him around town at various functions. He's gorgeous. And rich. Quite the catch, my dear boy. But honestly, he's the lucky one. I just hope he's good enough for you. When do I get to meet him?"

"Tomorrow. Brunch. Quarrel's. 11:00."

"It's a date. I can't wait to tell Ralph. It's what we've been wishing for all along for you. It's the answer to all our prayers."

Rain knew it was the answer to their prayers, as he had already envisioned the keys to the store being handed over to him. Was this what they'd been waiting for? For him to be settled before they could take off and live out their lives in retirement? They were waiting for him. He felt his throat start to close as the rush of emotion hit him. What amazing friends they were. Family. He would miss them so much.

✳ ✳ ✳

Brunch was perfect, and Gene welcomed Creighton like the prodigal son.

Then came the list of dos and don'ts.

"I know you're a wealthy man, Creighton Marlin, but money can't buy happiness. Although, it certainly can't hurt," Gene said as he finished off his eighth mimosa. "My Rainey here—"

"You never call me, 'Rainey,' Rain cut in, feeling no pain himself. "Only Ed calls me that. And he shouldn't either. I hate it. Geney." He chuckled. "Like I Dream of Geney."

"Yes, I know, Gene. As you've said, fifteen times, I believe. Rain is like a son to you and Ralph. I promise you he won't be hurt. I love him," Creighton said.

Gene pulled himself upright and cleared his throat. "Well then, why didn't you say that thirteen mimosas ago and I could have saved my breath. I'm getting old. I don't know how many breaths, or mimosas, I have left. He loves you, Rain."

"I know," Rain said.

"Well, you should have told me."

"I thought you knew. I didn't think I had to spell it out."

Gene nodded sagely as he said, "When it comes to love, it always has to be spelled out. L-O-V-E. It's the most important word in the world and not to be bandied about lightly. But I know you're an honest Southern gentleman and would never lie to another—older, more venerable—Southern gentleman... would you?"

He tapped Creighton on the nose, and Rain knew Gene had given his stamp of approval.

"I give you my word, as one Southern gentleman to another. I love this man, Rainier Cantrell, and will love him till death us do part."

Gene gave another firm nod. "Well, all right then. Let's have another round of mimosas and head to the shop. I've got a little surprise for you... Rainey." He laughed uproariously. Rain just tsked and gave a knowing look to Creighton.

✳ ✳ ✳

"As long as I'm here, I might as well do a little prophesized shopping." Creighton gave Rain a wink as he perused the store. "Do I get your employee discount?"

"Creighton Marlin with all your money you could buy my whole store and not bat one of those luscious eyes of yours," Gene said as he and Ralph appeared from the back room. "This is my partner, Ralph. I've told him everything about you." The older balding gentleman bowed slightly and took Creighton's proffered hand.

Creighton smiled warmly at him. "A pleasure, sir."

"And now for the surprise, Rain." Gene was effusive. "Here you go, my darling boy." He handed some documents to Rain. "The store is all yours, except for some 'i' dotting. May you enjoy it half as much as Ralph and I are going to enjoy our retirement in Hawaii."

Rain tried to look shocked, and actually he was a little. He hadn't envisioned Gene going to Hawaii. "I guess the details are left out sometimes," he told Creighton under his breath.

"I don't know what to say, gentlemen. I don't know what I'm going to do without you two," Rain said with genuine emotion.

"I'm sure you'll find something to occupy your time, till you get over your grieving at our departure." Gene winked at Creighton. "Besides, we'll be back to visit. I have to make sure this boy here takes good care of you and keeps his word." He tapped the last three words out on Creighton's nose.

"Yes, sir," Creighton said.

"And of course, now you'll have an excuse to come visit us in Hawaii," Ralph said, obviously excited at the prospect of their move. "And Creighton, you make sure Rain doesn't work too hard and you come at least twice a year to visit. I think that's in the contract."

"Really?" Rain said.

"No, but I think I'm going to add it," Gene said. "Good idea, Ralph, my sweet."

Creighton laughed. "We'll be there. I promise."

Gene went into the back again and appeared a moment later with a dark-colored bottle. "We need to celebrate, boys! Here's my thirty-five-year-old bourbon that I've been saving for just such an occasion. So, start tryin' on clothes and Ralph'll get the glasses."

The rest of the afternoon went by in a flurry. And after a lot of tears had been shed over numerous goodbyes, Rain and Creighton left to start their new lives together.

"We don't have to take them to the airport tomorrow," Rain said as Creighton drove slowly along. "I don't think I could handle any more goodbyes. Can you be hugged to death? And why are we going this way? This is the long way."

"That bourbon, while being as smooth as butter, really packed a wallop. I didn't want to drive through the crowded streets. You know Atlanta drivers. Besides, this way I can drive slowly and you can cuddle up next to me."

"And here I never knew you had this devious side. I like it," Rain said as he moved over next to Creighton and took his arm. "I like this car. It's got a bench seat. Perfect for cuddling."

"Why do you think I brought it out?" Creighton kissed him on the side of his head.

Bright lights.

"NOOOO!" Rain screamed. His thoughts immediately turned to his vision. This couldn't be happening. Not now. He thought everything would be all right, that his vision was something else. He was deluding himself. He'd felt the impending doom. Why hadn"t h listened? He was too in love. And now he'd probably killed them both.

The lights were upon them. Blinding. He screamed again as he felt a weight being pressed down upon him.

Creighton.

He'd covered him with his body and dragged him down.

Creighton, my love, I'm sorry. He felt a terrific jolt to his body.

Blackout.

* * *

Bright lights.

He closed his eyes.

"Rainey," a soft drawling voice said in his ear. "Come back. We're here for you. All of us: Gene and Ralph, and I even snuck in Little Eddy."

In response, Little Eddy gave a little yip.

"Hush now. You want to get us thrown out? Rainey, you had us so scared."

Rain tried opening his eyes again. The lights were still bright. He realized he must be in a hospital. He tried to speak. "Whaaa..." was all he could croak. His throat felt rough and dry.

"Ralph, raise the bed so I can give him something to drink. Here, Gene, hold Eddy for me please." Ed handed the dog off.

Rain tried to pull himself up and winced. His head ached. He slowly reached up to ease the throbbing and felt a large bandage covering the top of his head.

"You must've hit your head on the roof of the car or something. You had a concussion, you poor boy," Gene explained. "But other than that, you're fit as a fiddle. Creighton took most of the impact."

Creighton.

Where was he? Was he all right? Rain began to panic. He tried to rise up again. The pain was too much. He tried to speak. A moan.

"Here, Rainey. Drink some of my tea. It's not too hot. It'll help wet your whistle." Ed tilted the cup to Rain's lips.

He drank slowly. The warm bitterness eased the dryness of his tongue. He swallowed slowly, then sipped again. "Is he...?"

"He's goin' to be fine," Gene assured him. "How about a glass of water?"

"No. I want to..." Rain still couldn't make his voice work. He took the cup from Ed and finished it. He cleared his throat. It felt a little better. "I have to know. Everything. Now." He paused, swallowed. "Please."

He heard Gene's voice catch. "All right. Just calm down."

Rain shut his eyes, said a silent prayer. When he opened them he was staring into the empty tea cup. He let out a small gasp.

Gene rushed to him. "What is it? Are you all right? Ralph, get the doctor."

"No," Rain managed. "I... Never mind. Tell me."

"Well, as near as the police could figure. It seems the driver of the other vehicle fell asleep at the wheel. He's fine. Apparently God does watch out for fools. Anyway, he was goin' home after a very long drive from Chattanooga to see his family, fell asleep, and went into your lane."

"Creighton..." Rain urged.

"I'm gettin' to him. Well, the dear boy tried to protect you and covered you with his body."

Rain felt himself get dizzy.

"The impact was full on the front of the car. It, sort of, folded in. They had to pry the two of you out. You were both unconscious, locked in each other's arms." Gene paused.

Rain appreciated the even tone he was keeping as he reported the facts. The pedantic delivery was driving him insane though. "Gene, please, just tell me."

"The steering wheel was driven into Creighton's left side. It broke several ribs and punctured his lung. His left hip was thrown out of its socket, but they put it back in. They've set his ribs and the lung should heal as well."

Rain couldn't stand it. He knew there was more. Something bad. "Gene!" he shouted, tearing his throat.

"Oh Rain, I'm sorry. He's in a coma."

Rain collapsed back onto the pillow, trying not to pass out.

"They don't seem to know why," Gene continued. "He may have bumped his head on yours, but there's no apparent brain damage. He's just... out. Maybe your concussion came from that. It's just a guess. He'll come out of it, Rain." He squeezed Rain's hand, then added, "He's got to."

Rain's eyes were closed as he squeezed back hard on Gene's hand. He felt the tears running down his face from his closed eyes. He whispered, "He's got to."

✳ ✳ ✳

Two days later, after much pleading and crying from Rain, the doctor agreed that he could take a short walk and see Creighton, his small entourage with him; this time sans Little Eddy. It was one little bark too many.

They entered Creighton's room. Tubes and monitors were everywhere, but strangely, Creighton had a serene, almost beatific look on his face. A communal lump came to the group's throats.

Rain approached him. He reached out a hand to caress the handsome face. "You wonderful, crazy man. I know why you saved me. I would have done the same. You were just quicker. And bigger. You love me. I know that. And I love you. You have to know that."

Rain heard a communal sniff behind him. "But I'm okay now. So you can come back to me. We've got a lot of life to live. Together. I have a little confession to make to you, so I hope you can hear me. I sort of expurgated that first reading I did for you. I saw something, but it was vague and I wasn't sure what it meant. Now I think I know. I saw Ed and Gene and Ralph surrounding a little baby. We were there too, just watching them. But the looks on our faces were ones of pride. It was our baby Creighton. Our baby. I hope you like kids. I do. I need you. I love you so much."

He collapsed onto Creighton's body and sobbed. The other three, also with sympathetic tears, surrounded him and gave their love.

"Was it a boy?" barely a whisper.

The four men turned to Creighton's face. It was still.

Rain could barely speak. "Ed, Gene, Ralph, did you hear that?"

The three nodded. Ed said, "Oh my yes."

Creighton's eyes began to flutter. Rain moved his face up to him. "Creighton, I'm here. I'm here. Oh please, wake up."

Creighton's eyes slowly opened. "Are you an angel?"

Rain sobbed again and held his face against Creighton's. "Creighton, I was so afraid. But I knew you'd make it. You had to. Gene, Ralph, and Ed all said you would. They've been here the whole time. They've been so great."

"Get the doctor, Ralph," Gene directed.

"Right," Ralph said. "But I need another Kleenex."

"Here, I've got an extra hanky," Ed said, handing over what looked like a tatted doily.

"Thank you, I think, "Ralph said and left the room.

"You didn't answer me," Creighton said to Rain. "Is it a boy?"

* * *

Several weeks later, with Rain all healed and Creighton still nursing the occasional twinge from his healing ribs, they lay in Creighton's enormous bed, enjoying the feeling of holding each other, never forgetting or taking for granted what they had almost lost.

"Are you sure about adopting?" Rain asked, stroking Creighton's bare chest. We have our appointment tomorrow."

"My love, you already saw it in our future. Who am I to argue with that?"

"But I have to know this is what you want too."

"I have always dreamed of having a family with the man I love. You're making my dream come true."

"As you've made mine," Rain said, kissing a nipple.

"Naughty, Yankee. Are you tryin' to compromise my fine, upstanding, Southern sensibilities?"

"Uh huh." A longer nipple kiss.

"All right. The South is goin' to surrender this time, but I want you do one thing for me first." He reached over to the night table.

"What do you have there?" Some trepidation in Rain's voice.

Creighton turned back. "My teacup from last night. I want you to look. I want you know how much I trust you and believe in you, my love."

"Creighton, I don't want to. I know you trust me."

"Please. I know you're afraid. But after what we've come through, how could anything be worse?" He thrust the cup at Rain.

Rain hesitantly looked down. He hadn't done this since the hospital. Would it be the same?

Yes. There it was. Just like before.

Nothing.

Just a muddy mess of leaves.

He'd lost it. His visions were gone. He figured it must have been the concussion. How did he feel? No more gift. No more futures.

Fantastic. That's how he felt.

Normal. He could make his own life and let the future unfold as it should. For he knew his future was bright. He was in love with the most wonderful, loving man—and they were about to adopt a child. A boy. Just like he'd seen. Life didn't get any better.

"I see..." he began. "Us. Smiling. Laughing. At the beach. At Disney World. Our son. Merry Christmases. Happy New Year. A lifetime of happiness."

"See. I told you."

"Yes, you did," Rain said, snuggling closer. "And I also saw us making love. Many, many times."

"Then we'd better get started," Creighton said, turning fully into him. "Because we know your visions always come true."

"Yes, they do."

SAGITTARIUS

The Archer–Half-Man, Half-Horse

Traits: Impulsive, Inquisitive, Likes change and Travel, Good-humored, Straight-forward, Optimistic, Freedom-loving.

"All right! I'll tell you what happened," Colton James said as he tossed back his third whiskey shot and took a sip on his fourth beer. "You boys do your shots too."

"We can't drink like you can. We need to be coherent for the semi-finals tomorrow." This came from Bo Jenkins, a scruffy, but charming, cowboy and calf roper and partner to Jed Randall, the wiry cowboy seated next to him.

"No drinky, no story," Colton said and toasted the boys.

Jed clinked glasses with the other two. "This better be worth it."

Colton took another swig of beer as the boys downed their shots, and he began, "He was just about the best looking guy I've ever seen. He coulda been the love of my life—"

"Coulda been?" Bo interrupted.

"Shush, Bo." And Jed elbowed his partner in the ribs.

"Oof!" Bo grunted. "Okay, Casanova, tell us how you managed to fu—Oof!" Another jab in the ribs from Jed. "Fouled this one up." He gave Jed a smirk.

"Well, I told him—"

"Wait, Colt!" Jed interrupted him this time. "From the beginning. We want all the juicy details."

"Then we're gonna need another shot. "Billy!" Colton yelled to their waiter and made the "another round" motion in the air.

The two boys groaned. "Colt!"

"This'll be worth it, boys. I think I outdid myself this time."

"That would be hard," Bo quipped. "Remember that Italianish calf roper at last year's Nationals?"

"Yeah. Joey Fillipo," Colt said, chagrined.

Bo started laughing, recalling the event. "There you were at dinner, getting all romantic and cow-eyed and then you drop your rib bone in your beer. And then, with total class, shoved your fist into the glass to get it out but instead dumped the beer all over the table and Joey!" Bo was howling now.

Jed joined in. "It was pretty classic Colton James fu—screw up. A word of advice, big guy. You might not ought to order messy finger food on a first date. Uh, uh. Baaad first impression."

"No shit," Colt grumbled. "I can't help it. You know I get nervous every time I'm around a guy I'm interested in. Besides, you two were only a couple of tables away from us. Why didn't you tell me not to order ribs? That's what you were there for, to make sure I didn't screw up, not to sit there and laugh your fool asses off when I almost dumped the whole table over!"

Jed and Bo were both laughing heartily now. "But you shoulda seen your face!" Bo yelled.

"No, you shoulda seen Joey's!" Jed added. "I never saw a guy hightail it out of a place so fast in my life!"

"Are you two through?" Colt gave them a glower. "You guys can laugh all you want. You've been together for ten years. But I'm thirty-three years old, with no prospects in sight!" He paused. "And here's our shots."

The waiter set the shots in front of them and gave Colton a wink.

Colt smiled back. "Thanks, Billy." And to the boys said, "Drink up, dicks."

"Aw, Colt," Bo whined. "You know we love you. But some of the dumb things you do with guys are just down right hilarious!"

"Enough, Bo," Jed said. "Go ahead, Colt. Tell us all about Mr. Wonderful."

"Shot first," Colt said. "For laughing at me."

They tossed the shots back and Colt began. "Well, it was Wednesday night, the first night of the prelims, and I decided I needed a drink or two to numb the pain in my butt after I fell hard that afternoon."

"Yeah, I was wonderin' how your butt was after that," Bo piped in. "It was a great ride though, and you seemed to be sittin' fine, so I guessed sex'd be okay too."

"Bo, must you?" Jed chided.

"Thanks for thinkin' of my sex life, Bo." Sarcasm from Colt. "But the only saddle I'll be back on again is my horse after my major screw up that night."

"Yeah?" Bo urged.

"Anyways, I'm wanderin' the room, drinkin' my drink, and I look over and there he is sittin' at the end of the bar drinkin' some pink thing."

"Ooo, bad sign." Bo shook his head.

"Bo!" Jed glared at him.

"Do you guys wanna hear my horror story or not?" Colt was getting exasperated.

"Sorry, Colt. Bo won't say another word. Will you!" Another glare from Jed and Bo silently zipped his mouth and winked at Colt.

"So he's sittin' there in his starched, white western shirt, designer jeans, and these very highly polished boots, which probably cost more than a month's mortgage on my ranch! I was standin' right over there by the pool table when he looked right at me. I thought I'd been struck by a bolt of lightning. He had these deep, deep-blue eyes and dark, dark hair. Black Irish I guess. This smooth, beautiful face and square jaw. He's probably thirty or so. And I give him my best hundred watt smile... and he turns away! Like I was a ogre or somethin'. And I hadn't even done nothin' stupid yet."

Jed shook his head in disbelief. "Whoa! That killer smile didn't work? Did you have spinach in your teeth or somethin'?"

"No. I just figured I wasn't his type, you know? But I wasn't gonna give up. Hell, he hadn't even shook my hand yet!"

"And that's a bad thing?" Bo mumbled. Jed flashed his eyes at him.

"So for once I thought I'd play it cool. I'd play a little pool and keep an eye on him. And guess what?"

"What?" the boys chorused.

"It worked! I would look over from time to time during the game an' I'd see him look at me and then glance away. He was interested. So, I acted all nonchalant like, while he nursed that pink thing he was drinkin'. I did get nervous once, though. He got up from the bar and I thought he was leavin', but he was just goin' to the little boy's room. And then he came back. An' I gotta tell you guys, you shoulda seen him when he stood up. Those jeans he was wearin' musta been handsewn, 'cuz they fit that tight little butt like a glove. And that package in the front was mighty impressive, too. As a matter of fact, those jeans caused me to sink the eight ball by accident! So, when he came back, I decided I better go for it before somebody else did. He caused quite a stir in those tight little jeans as he passed through the bar. And nobody else'd shown up to join him, tho' I'd seen him shove off a couple of guys earlier. I said to myself, now's the time."

"Colt? Can this wait just a sec'. I gotta pee real bad."

Jed growled, "Hold it, Bo."

"I was just kiddin'. I thought we needed a tension breaker." Which got him another jab in the rib cage.

Colt continued. "So I strode over to the bar, planted myself on the stool next to him, and said, 'Can I buy you a drink? My name's Colt.' I thought his neck was gonna snap he turned to me so fast! And he didn't say anything. So I turned to the bartender and told him to bring us two more of whatever he'd been drinkin'. Then he says to me, 'My name's Ryland McAuliffe–Ry,' he told me to call him. And he gave me the cutest little half-smile... God! He was cute! I gave him my hand and he shook it, and I asked him what he did, and he said somethin' about land investments and how he was here lookin' at some land here up north. And then I asked him how he liked the rodeo. And he said he loved it. And then I said, I thought I seen him sittin' up in those expensive seats in the stands—"

"Uh, oh," Bo said.

"Bo..." Jed warned.

"Sorry. But it was kind of gauche to say that, you know."

"I know. I realized it after I'd said it. But I wanted him to know I'd noticed him. Besides, he seemed to like it that I had noticed him. So there."

"Then what happened?" Jed said, warily.

"Everything went to shit!" Colt slapped his hands on the table and would have knocked over his beer if Jed hadn't been quick enough to grab it. "But it wasn't my fault! At least not all of it."

"What... happened... Colt?" Jed prodded.

"Well, he started it." Colt was petulant now. "I was smart. I excused myself and got up and went to the bathroom so I could think up somethin' to say next, before I said another dumb thing. And when I came back the first thing he says to me is—and I swear to God this is the truth—he says, 'So, what's your sign?'"

"No!" the boys chorused again.

"What decade is he living in?"

"You shoulda run for the hills, pardner." Jed waited for Colt to respond. "But you didn't, did you?"

Colt was stone-faced.

"What did you do, Colt?"

"Jed, he was so cute. I just couldn't leave. So I... I..."

"You what?"

"I said, 'I'm a Sagittarius. The centaur. You know, half man, half horse." Colt gritted his teeth. "Then I sorta spread my legs apart and said..." He gulped. "Guess which part's the horse?"

"No!" Bo.

"You didn't!" Jed.

"Yup. I did." Colt hung his head.

Bo broke the silence. "So, what'd he say?"

"Nuthin. He... uh... looked at my crotch, turned the color of a stop light, and turned away."

"Well, I would guess he would!" Bo exclaimed. Everybody knows about the famous member of Colton James!" A few heads in the bar turned in their direction, as the band had stopped playing a few minutes before, and Bo was anything but discreet.

"Enough, Bo!" Jed yelled. "And you're drunk."

"So?" Bo pouted. "It's true."

"Well shit, guys! It's not like I'm a freak or anything. It's not that big!" Colt looked around. A few more ears had tuned in.

"Have you looked in the mirror lately? Were you wearin' those jeans?" Bo raised his eyebrows.

Colt nodded.

"No wonder he ran."

"I said, enough, Bo!" Jed shoved him hard. "Apologize."

"Aw, I'm sorry, Colt," Bo said contritely, then whispered, "But it is big. And don't hit me again, Jed! Remember, I'm your ropin' partner. You need me."

"Yeah, well that could change." Jed turned to Colt. "I'm sorry, Colt. You'll–"

"There's more." Colt had bowed his head again.

"More?" Bo perked up.

"I kinda mumbled an 'I'm sorry.' And he said 'That's okay. I'm a Sagittarius too... the centaur, half horse...' And he turned stop-light red again."

"Sounds like a match made in heaven... or somewhere." Bo quipped.

"Yeah," Colt said. "I wish. Then he says he just meant that it was his sign and we're compatible, and that made him blush more. It was adorable. And if the way those jeans fit him was any indication, he might be half horse down there too." He finished off his beer and wiped his mouth before continuing. "Then he apologized again for even asking about my sign, but that he was nervous 'cuz I'm such a great rider and famous... and just when I thought maybe there was a chance... the drinks showed up."

"That's bad? Did you spill 'em or something?"

"Worse."

"Worse?" the boys in harmony again.

"Worse. I raised my glass to toast and I said, 'Here's to our signs. I hope they're compatible.'"

"Hey, that was pretty good, Colt." Bo nodded in admiration.

"Then I took a swallow... and spit it out all over him!"

"Colt!" The boys gaped in shock.

Bo gathered himself together first. "That's a new low. Even for you."

Jed tried to be more understanding. "What happened? Was it poisoned or somethin'?"

"Naw, it just tasted like shit."

"So what'd you do?" Colt stared at Bo, who was like a kid at his first horror movie. All he needed was popcorn.

"I grabbed a bunch of napkins off the bar and started to wipe him off. I didn't even realize I was rubbing up and down on his crotch till he said, 'Maybe I should clean up down there.' And my hand froze and I realized he had a big ole hard-on goin' on. Here he is with this pink shit drippin' off his face and all over his $300, white-as-snow shirt, and he's got this ragin' hard-on!"

"God! This just gets better and better." Bo was now leaning halfway across the table. "Then what?"

"Then he reached down and pulled my hand away and said, 'I'll just go to the wash room.' Then I hear Mikey from behind the bar say, 'Too bad, Colt. I thought you had a keeper.' I wanted to run outta there so bad, but I couldn't 'cuz I had to pay him for his shirt. So then he comes back and tells me he'd better go back to the hotel and change, and I try to apologize and offer to pay for his shirt, but he refuses and says it's his fault for wearing white. Then he says, "Oh by the way, it's campari and soda. I don't like it either. But I order it so that I'll drink it slowly, then I won't get too drunk and make a fool of myself, but I guess it's too late for that.' And then he left. Can you believe it! He takes the blame for me screwing up! He's perfect! And I am the biggest..."

"Fuck up!" They chorused as a trio.

"Thanks, guys. I knew I could count on you to cheer me up."

"I think you should see him again," Jed announced. "You're perfect for one another. The attraction is obviously there. And you're both socially inept..."

"And their signs are compatible." Bo couldn't resist. "And their dicks—"

"Are you guys nuts? He probably doesn't even want to see me from the stands. Let alone on a date."

"Colt, you never know. If you see him again, at least you'll have passed the curse of the first date," Jed reasoned.

"It wasn't a date. I tried to pick him up."

"First encounter then. You aren't good with those either."

"Thanks, Jed. You make me feel a whole lot better about myself." Colt grinned wistfully. "But I sure would like another chance. There was something special about him. I knew it when his eyes first met mine across the room."

"Across a crowded room,

"And somehow you know,

"You know even then..." Bo sang.

Colt and Jed stared. Stunned.

"You know, guys, *Some Enchanted Evening. South Pacific?* Hello! Gay! Broadway musical!"

"We know, Bo. We just can't believe you would start singing a show tune at the top of your lungs in a country bar."

"Come on, Jed. Everybody's gay here. They all know it."

"That's it, Bo. It's time to go. Come on, Colt. Drink up. We'll walk back to the hotel with you." Jed and Bo rose to leave.

"Naw, you guys go. I don't have to ride till late tomorrow. I think I'll just sit here and drown my sorrows and try to figure out why I'm such a loser."

"Aw, Colt. You're not a loser." Bo came back to the table and hugged him. "You're just... just..."

"A fuck up," Colt finished for him. "Thanks, Bo."

"Anytime, Colt."

Jed grabbed Bo. "Good night, Colt."

As they left, Colt signaled for another beer and a shot.

"May I join you?"

Colt looked up... and into midnight blue eyes.

Time stopped. Colt drank in the sight: a perfectly tailored vermillion shirt; perfectly tailored tight, black jeans; a black cowboy hat; and a mind-numbing little half smile.

Colt nodded.

Ryland McAuliffe, the man of perfection that Colt thought he would never see again, slid into the booth opposite him and tossed his hat up on the back of it. "I have to confess something."

Colt didn't respond. He was spellbound.

"I saw you and your friends when I came in and I didn't want to intrude, so I sat in the booth right here behind you. I was trying to think of a way to break into the conversation, but I... didn't. I'm sorry... I... It was wrong. I mean, to eavesdrop like that. I shouldn't have... Are you going to say something?"

"You look great."

"Thanks. Uh, you do, too."

"Naw. I look like shit. I'm drunk. You look great."

"Here's your drink, Colt." The waiter eyed Ryland. "Would you like something?" The double entendre was obvious.

"I'll have what he's having. It's safer." Ryland grinned.

Colt now grinned, too, getting the meaning of the statement. "Did you wear the red shirt just in case?"

Ryland relaxed a little now. "No. And I told you I shouldn't have worn white. I've also sworn off campari and soda. Thank you."

The waiter returned with the drinks.

"That was quick," Colt noted.

"Inspiration," the waiter said and smiled at Ryland.

"So what am I drinking here?" Ryland studied the mug and the shot glass sitting in front of him. "I figured I should ask, since the last time it didn't work out so well with the mystery drink."

Colt bristled slightly at this. "I told you I'm sorry. I—"

"Hey, I was joking. I just thought if we laughed about it we could forget it and move on."

Move on? Was there a chance? Colt hoped like hell there was.

"It's called a boiler maker." Colt raised the shot glass. This is a shot of rye and you're supposed to drop it in the beer and then drink it. But, as I am socially inept and a klutz, as my dear friends tell me, I choose to drink the shot and chase it with the beer."

"Sounds like the smart way to go. I'm sure I would also make a mess of dropping it in the glass."

"To you, Ry. Thanks for giving me another shot. I think a shot of Ry is just what I need." Colt tossed the shot back, wondering if his Ry puns had been too much.

Ry also downed his shot, then raised his beer mug. "I love how you say whatever you feel. It's very refreshing. Please, let me try to do the same. I've never been good at it. To you, Colt. You make me feel like there's hope and goodness still out there and that it can be wrapped in a great package." His face reddened and he swiftly drank his beer.

Colt grinned from ear to ear, noting the "package" comment, and prodded, "You have to drink the whole beer at once. That's it... a little more..."

Ry slammed down the empty mug and Colt quickly followed.

"That's my little cowboy." Colt grinned again.

Ry raised an eyebrow. Colt thought that maybe he shouldn't have said little.

He flashed a smile at Ry, and he responded. "I'm 5'9. Not that little."

Yup. Shouldn't have said little. When will I ever learn? Colt chuckled. "No, you're not. I didn't mean it that way. I was just tryin' to be—"

"It's all right. I kind of liked it."

Their eyes locked and the world around them froze. It was magic. It was destiny. It was...

"This round's on me, boys. And I get off at two." The waiter dropped the drinks and trailed away.

"I think he's looking for a three-way," Colt said. "But I'm not sharing."

"Me either."

They both froze and blushed at the same time.

Ry broke the awkwardness, but his voice was a little higher pitched than usual. "Colt, I'm really bad at this. I... I... I need another drink." He bolted his shot down and followed it just as quickly with the beer. Colt just stared. "And I have to tell you one other thing about me, which will probably make you hightail it out of here. You know when I asked you your sign—your zodiac sign?" He barreled on, not waiting for a response. "I'm kind of into astrology. I do horoscopes and I follow what they tell me. For example, I was supposed to go out and meet people—that was the night we first met—and my horoscope told me I would meet—and I'm not making this up–a tall, dark-eyed man with whom I could become romantically involved. Watch for Pisces and... Sagittarius. That's you. So, when you told me your sign, and I already knew who you were, of course, and I thought you were great looking... so I thought you were the one. Now, I'm scared I told you all that. Please don't run off. It really works. I use it for investments and deals, and it's paid off. I've made shitloads of money from it. Sorry, I didn't mean to say shitloads. I'm babbling, I know. But I wanted you to know that about me. I never tell other people this because I think it would freak them out. But please believe me, the stars don't lie. You just have to know how to read them. Please say something, Colt, or I might start to cry or something. I really like you."

"I know I'm shitfaced, but I think I'm in love." Colt tossed back his shot, raised his beer mug, and leaned on his hands, staring at the handsome buck caught in the headlights. "Now don't be scared. I say that every time I meet a cute guy I like. Maybe that's why I'm single." He drank.

Ry seemed totally befuddled.

"I think I need the little boy's room." Colt got up from the seat and immediately fell to the floor.

Ry rushed to him immediately, not feeling too steady himself.

"Colt! Colt! Are you all right? Say something!"

Colt raised his head. "You're beautiful." And passed out.

* * *

Ry got the waiter to help him get Colt into a cab and took him to his hotel. He had no idea which hotel Colt was staying in, so his had seemed like the logical choice.

They arrived at Ry's hotel, and as the doorman opened the taxi door, it happened.

Ten beers and almost as many shots of rye spewed forth. Colt covered himself and the back of the cab.

Ry was horrified but unscathed. "I'm so sorry," he told the cabbie, who was now ranting from the front seat in a Russian dialect. "Here, I'll pay for it." And he thrust a wad of bills over onto the front seat.

The cabbie looked at the bills and instantly calmed. The doorman had also thankfully appeared with a large towel and handed it to Ry.

Ry wiped Colt down as much as he could and removed him from the cab. Colt, barely coherent, clung on to Ry.

Another doorman miraculously appeared with a wheelchair and helped Colt into it. Ry couldn't help but thinking how grateful he was to be staying at a five-star hotel where "guest service" reigned supreme—no matter the situation. And this definitely was above and beyond the call of duty. He drew some more bills from his pocket and thrust them at the attendants. "Thank you so much. I'm sorry. My friend... ate some bad sushi.... I... thank you. He'll be fine." And he quickly wheeled Colt into the hotel.

As they neared the door to Ry's suite, Colt stirred. "I'm sorry, Ry." He paused. "But I think I feel better."

"You will feel better after we get you cleaned up and into bed." Ry slid the key card into the lock.

Colt struggled to his feet. "Bed sounds good. Are you going to join me?"

Ry pushed the door open. "There's one bathroom here on the right. I'll use the other one in the master." He was proud of himself for ignoring Colt's invitation. But he couldn't help feeling a slight thrill of anticipation, although he knew it was futile. There was no way this cowboy would be riding anything tonight. He smiled at the image that summoned. "If you need me, just call."

"Oh, I'll be needing you all right." Colt slapped Ry's butt as he left the room.

Ry was stunned and as aroused as he could be. This was just too surreal.

Ry cleaned himself up and was just about to don a pair of boxers to sleep in. He usually slept in the nude, but he did have a guest. Guest. Some guest. The hottest man on the planet. Vomit and all.

"I see you're ready for me."

Ry whirled toward the doorway, his boxers flew in the same direction and landed at Colt's feet. He eyed Ry's crotch. "I may have some competition here. You won't be needing these." Colt bent down, picked up Ry's boxers and tossed them over his shoulder.

Ry's jaw dropped. He stared at the nude and fully aroused form of a god. His first thought was. It's true. He is half horse!

"I'm glad you like what you see. I'm all yours." Colt opened his arms as he approached Ry. "God, you're gorgeous." He embraced Ry and pulled him down to the bed. "Can I kiss you? I brushed my teeth. I think I used your toothbrush. Sorry."

Ry had never heard anything so sexy in his life. This incredible hunk had just asked if he could kiss him! And he had used his toothbrush. He didn't think he could get any harder... but he did.

Colt hovered over him waiting for an answer. Those dark smoldering eyes waiting for his response. "Please."

The lips that covered his seemed to melt every bone in his body. Ry tasted mint and whisky and... Colt, that innate taste that was this incredible man. It was more intoxicating than the finest Napoleon brandy. He parted his lips and drank fully. Colt covered his mouth and body with his own. Every square inch of flesh was seared. This wasn't just kissing, it was melding. Two entities joining to become one. Ry had longed for this his entire life. He'd had faith that it was out there. His horoscope hadn't lied; it never did. It told him about meeting a big man who would change his life. Colton James. Ry mused, did my horoscope mean this kind of big?

All Ry's senses were on fire. The kiss just seemed to go on and on. And he got more and more lost in it.

Then the kiss slowed and stopped. Colt's mouth was pressed to his, but there was no movement. Ry tried to move his mouth for a response, but got none. He wriggled his face away from Colt's. "Colt? Colt? Are you okay? Colt?"

Colt's eyes were closed. His mouth slightly open. His breathing was deep. Colt had fallen asleep.

Ry was stunned. Then, resigned, he tried to extricate himself from beneath Colt.

He had just managed to get beside him when he felt himself drawn back and locked into two brawny arms. Ry thought, perhaps, that Colt had awakened, but no, he had just repositioned. Ry's face was in Colt's chest. He could feel the light dusting of hair brushing his cheek. It was glorious. Well, at least he was warm and comfortable and... hard. But it was worth it. He would rather be asleep in this man's arms than any other place in the world or with any other man.

This was the best night of his life.

* * *

Colt opened his eyes and stared at the empty pillow next to him. There was a piece of paper on it. He raised his head a little and immediately put it back down. He was hung-over.

What had he had to drink? His eyes scanned his hotel room. This wasn't his hotel room. Where was he? He grabbed the paper.

Breakfast should arrive at 11:00. Your clothes should also be done around that time. If not, you can borrow whatever you'd like. At least the socks and underwear should fit. Don't worry about the room. The maid staff should have taken care of everything by the time you wake up. If you would like to use the hotel gym or spa, I have made arrangements for you.

And if you would like a massage, just let the staff know. They have your name. I have a meeting until late afternoon, but I should make it for your ride. I believe it's at 4:00. If you don't have any plans this evening, would you like to go to dinner with me? If you're busy, I understand. If not, the restaurant at the top of the Stratosphere is very nice. The food is good and the view is spectacular. I made a reservation for 8:00. If you can make it, great, if not it's all right. I understand. But I will be there waiting. Good luck today on your ride, but you don't need it. You're the best. Thank you for last night.

Ry

Ry. He remembered. Ugh! He remembered. All the gory details. The bar. The cab. The cab. Oh, how could he have gotten sick. He never got sick. He remembered more now. The bathroom. The shower. The bedroom. Ry. The bedroom! A kiss. An incredible kiss. He had devoured Ry in a kiss like no other he had ever experienced. He remembered his mind exploding with sensation. He remembered getting lost and being transported to another plane of existence. He remembered... what? What had happened next? They'd made love, of course. But why couldn't he remember it? That kiss had been mind-blowing. Surely the sex had been even better. Why couldn't he remember? It would come to him. He knew it would, after he woke up and had something to eat. Some coffee. He needed some coffee.

Then as if by willing it, the doorbell rang. He sprang up from the bed and went to the door. He reached for the knob and... he was naked. He called through the door. "Just a minute." He ran into the front room's bath for a towel. And carelessly throwing it around his waist, he rushed back to the door.

"Just put it anywhere," he gestured to the man as the cart was wheeled into the room. And as he gestured, the precariously draped towel dropped to the floor.

The man eyed Colt up and down, his eyes stopping just below Colt's waist. "Anything else I can do for you?"

Colt smirked. "I can handle it myself."

"Very good, sir. But I am very good at handling big problems if they should arise."

"I'm sure you are. And I'll let your manager know just how accommodating you can be."

The man nodded.

"As you can see, I don't have any change on me, so I'll have to catch you later."

The man stiffened slightly. "Very good, sir." And left the room.

"Bo and Jed are just gonna love this one." He moved to the cart and poured the coffee.

The doorbell rang again.

He opened the door. "I told you I can handle—"

"Eee!" A woman screamed.

"Shit!" I'm sorry. Just a minute. I thought you were... He closed the door, grabbed the towel from the floor and knotted it at his waist.

"I'm sorry... I—"

"Your laundry, sir." The short, dark-haired woman held the clothes out in front of her while averting her gaze.

Colt grabbed the hangers from her. "Thanks. I'll get ya later. Sorry again, ma'am."

He threw his clothes on a couch and returned to his coffee, muttering, "With all my screwups, I'll never figure out how I can be a bronc rider." He sipped his coffee, then screamed, "I have a date!"

✳ ✳ ✳

As Colt mounted his horse, he kept thinking about Ry and praying he would be watching him from the stands... or box. How had he gotten so lucky? This gorgeous... rich... guy, liked him—even after he'd spit up on him and then thrown up on him. Or close to it. Maybe the guy was a freak. Or weirdo. Or was into some really kinky stuff. Naw. He'd seemed so nice and normal and hung and... hot. Just thinking about him was making him hard. What a kisser. What a... He still couldn't remember the sex.

What was wrong with him? Had it been that bad? Had it been that boring? Maybe he slept... Oh great God in heaven, no! Had he fallen asleep? He couldn't have, could he? With that incredibly hot, perfect, awesome guy? No. Not even he could screw up that much. Could he?

✳ ✳ ✳

He was off. The horse bucked beneath him as the crowd yelled and he bucked up and down. Eight seconds. It seemed like such a short time. But when you were on the back of a bucking horse or bull, it was eternity. He held on for dear life and tried to scan the boxes in hopes of a glimpse of his beloved Ry. Beloved? Where had that come from? He didn't even use words like that. Hell! He'd just met the guy. And only kissed him once. But it was an amazing kiss. He hadn't even had sex with him. But did he need to? This guy might just be it. He couldn't see if Ry was watching him. Wasn't he done yet? The clowns were yelling something and waving their arms. Get off! Was he done?

He jumped off the bronc and scooted to the side. The clowns escorted him away. The wranglers went after the horse. The crowd was screaming something.

"Colt! Colt! Colt!"

They were chanting his name. He must have done well. Good. But had Ry been there to see him? 8: 00 P.M. The Stratosphere restaurant. The Top of the World. That was appropriate. He was on top of the world. He was in love.

* * *

8:00 P.M.

Ry sat in the lounge of The Top of the World restaurant. He'd been there since 7:30 in case Colt showed up early. His horoscope chart had told him he needed to be early and ready for anything today, to be prepared and patient and he would be able to deal with anything. It had certainly proven true at his meeting. He'd been early, they'd been late, and while they'd fumbled with excuses about traffic, Ry had his proposal on the table and they were signing the dotted line. They had agreed to a deal that would make Ry millions, and in all fairness it would benefit them as well. Ry would take advantage of a situation but would never take advantage of a person or, in this case, a company. It wasn't him. His shark instincts smelled his prey but never devoured. He sipped his water and checked his Rolex. He called the waiter over and ordered a bourbon on the rocks. He was so nervous. He'd needed to calm down. The bourbon would help.

8:02. Colt wasn't going to show. This was Colton James. The rodeo king, for God's sake. He could have anybody. But he had said, "I think I'm in love," to him. Of course, then he'd said that he said that to all the guys he liked and thought were cute. But at least that meant he liked him and thought he was cute. Aargh. He must be crazy. But that ride Colt had made today. Eleven seconds! Unbelievable. And it looked like he could have gone on for hours. Ry had never seen anything like it. The crowd had gone wild, but Colt had seemed almost oblivious to it, as if he were somewhere else and not on the back of a crazed bucking stallion. He'd been so proud of Colt. Not that he had any real attachment to him—other than one unimaginable kiss. Still, he was proud that he knew him. But now it looked as though that's all it would be: one incredible kiss. One night of bliss, sleeping in the arms of the most amazing man he had ever met. One memory that would have to last him a lifetime. And it would. But what if there were more? What if he could be with Colt for the rest of their lives? His horoscope was not telling him anything. Follow your instincts. That had been too vague. Did it mean with business or with Colt? Or both? He was so confused. He was usually so certain and straightforward with his thinking. Colt had cast some kind of spell over him, and now he didn't know what or whom to trust. He wished he had his chart in front of him. He must have missed something. For the first time in his life Ry wasn't certain of his interpretation of his chart. What if he'd lost his gift? What if...?

There he was. Colton James stood at the entryway of the lounge. He wore a cream-colored shirt, dark pants, a chocolate blazer, and a cowboy bolo tie. His longish, wavy, dark blond hair was just messed enough to give him the sexiest, most rakish look Ry had ever seen. Dark eyes scanned the room and met deep blue ones. Time froze. And like magnets the blue and brown eyes were drawn to one another.

* * *

Across a crowded room, my ass! Colt thought, as he approached who he thought was the most perfect man on earth.

Ry wore a sky-blue shirt, casually unbuttoned at the neck, navy pants, and a matching jacket. His eyes were deeper blue and more intense than ever. Colt now understood the meaning of the term "smoldering eyes." He felt as if he were walking to his destiny.

* * *

"I'm glad you could come," Ry said, and then immediately wanted to retract the words. "I mean, I'm glad you could make it." Aah. What was he doing? "Colt, that was an incredible ride today. I've never seen anythi–"

And then he was being kissed. Right there. In public. In the middle of the lounge at the Stratosphere Hotel, in Las Vegas, Nevada! Colton James, the rodeo king, was kissing him, Ryland McAuliffe. And he was kissing him back.

Colt broke the kiss. "Thank you."

Ry's eyes were still rolling. "For what?"

"For being you."

Ry couldn't respond. He could only stare. Who was this man? Who was he that could turn his world completely around and totally mesmerize him? Make him forget where he was and what he was doing. Make him open up and not care what he was doing, or who he was doing it with. Was this love? He could only hope so. Ry pulled Colt to him and pressed his mouth to his. "Ditto."

After the short but scorching kiss, Colt broke away and laughed loudly, causing the heads to turn–that already weren't turned–toward them. He pulled Ry down to the chairs and said, "Are you drunk?"

"Yes, but not in the way you mean."

Colt laughed again. "I think we're causing a scene, my little cowboy."

"I think they're jealous. Would you like a drink before dinner?"

"Can I share yours?"

Emboldened by the alcohol, Ry responded, "We can share whatever you'd like," and handed Colt his drink.

"I hope you know what you're getting into." Colt knocked back the rest of the drink.

"I hope you know what I hope we're getting into."

"You can't be drunk if you can spit out phrases like that. I'm not sure I know what you meant."

"Good. It'll give me time to figure it out, too. I hope you're hungry. They have great steaks and great desserts."

Colt leered. "I know what I want for dessert."

Ry could feel himself blush. Emboldening was over.

"I made you blush." Colt shook his head in amazement. "If you just aren't the sweetest, cutest..." He lowered his voice. "...sexiest thing I've ever seen. Can we just go right to dessert? 'Cuz if I stand up right now, I'm gonna cause a real scene."

"I think we should wait here a while. There are some elderly people here that just might not be prepared for such a... big surprise," Ry said, regaining a little bravado.

"Which reminds me, about last nigh—"

"Colt, you don't have to apologize for anything. It happens to the best of us. That's what friends are for. And I hope we are friends..."

"We are. But I have to ask you something, even though I may wreck everything. We kissed, right?"

"Yes." Ry was getting a little nervous.

"And it was amazing?"

"Yes."

"Good. I thought so, too. But you know I was a little drunk."

"Just a little."

"Thanks for that. I just wondered how much I dreamed and how much was—"

"Colt, stop. We kissed. You pulled me into your arms and we fell asleep together. We were both exhausted and... a little... intoxicated, and we fell asleep. Is that what you remember?"

"Yeah." His eyes moistened. "You're really somethin', you know that?"

"Ready to eat?"

"Yeah. Let's get to it. I'm lookin' forward to the best dessert I've ever had!"

∗ ∗ ∗

"My father was a bank investor and I became a land investor, much to my father's disappointment," Ry said between bites of filet mignon.

"Disappointment?"

"My father and I disagreed over everything: books, movies, the horoscope… my sexual preferences. Especially my sexual preferences. My parents had a beautiful, suitable girl all picked out for me. She was very nice and rich and smart, but still a girl. My father didn't get it. He thought I was just being stubborn. Can you believe it? This genius in the banking world thought that I said I was gay just to be stubborn."

"That's kinda pathetic, you know." Colt wagged a fork at Ry. "My folks were great about it. They loved me and just wanted me to find someone who was worthy of me." He felt his eyes begin to mist up. "God, I miss them. It's been six years for Mom and five for Dad. He was kinda lost without her. Now, I just work the ranch by myself and rodeo."

"How do you find the time?"

"Oh, I've got some hands that help me out with the horses and watch things while I'm on the road. That's why I only go to the bigger events. Fortunately, I'm the best in the business and I can rack up my points with fewer rodeos." Colt popped another piece of steak in his mouth. "You're right, this steak is great. And I'm just kinda braggin' about bein' the best. I'm sure there're some other fellers out there almost as good." He gave a huge grin to Ry and chuckled.

Ry tried to recover from the devastating smile. "But you are the best, Colt. I've watched you for years—"

"You have, have you? Then how come I've never seen you before? I certainly woulda remembered a guy as hot as you." He took a big gulp of his red wine.

Ry was silent while Colt drank, then said, "I was afraid."

Colt sputtered. "Of me?"

"Yup." Ry tried to ease his squeamishness by imitating Colt's accent.

"Now that may be the dumbest, sweetest, thing I've ever heard." Colt grinned a wide-eyed smile.

"Well, you were this rodeo king, and I'm just this boring land investor, and everyone loves you and wants you and—"

"Don't I wish. Drink your cabernet or whatever it is, and I'll tell you a little secret. I'm scared shitless of guys and relationships and love and stuff. I know I'm okay to look at and all that, but when I get around guys that are cute and, I don't know... I choke. I can't just be happy-go-lucky, fun-lovin' me. I think I've gotta be somebody more responsible and mature and—Shit! I don't know. Jed and Bo have helped me a lot, but it doesn't seem to make any difference. Each date is more a nightmare than the next. It gets depressing. And I hate being depressed. There, now you know. You can run for the hills anytime, but I gotta tell one more thing."

Ry was silent.

"I can't afford to pay the bill. My credit card is maxxed. I hope you've got plenty of money. This ain't gonna be cheap. I guess you pay for this incredible view. I mean, you can see the whole valley from up here. The strip, downtown—"

Ry couldn't help but burst into a wild peal of laughter.

Colt stared for a moment than began to laugh himself. All his anxieties seemed to be gone at once.

After their laughter died, Colt said, "I do have one more thing to say. And it's how I feel. I never believe in holding things back, but I guess you figgered that out by now."

"Yup."

Colt grinned. "I never met anyone like you. You really listen and care. It's like you can see through all this 'rodeo king' bullshit and see... me. And maybe I never had a successful relationship or anything with anyone 'cuz I never found the right guy. Maybe I should've been reading my horoscope. You say it works for you." He stared into dark blue pools and had never felt so vulnerable or scared in his life.

* * *

Ry didn't know what to say. He knew what he wanted to say, but he just couldn't. What if he was wrong? He could get hurt. Of course, that was better than being alone for the rest of his life. What would his father say? Fuck his father. This was his life. He wanted to get out of investing and just settle down somewhere and... live. God knew he had enough money. Money. He began to laugh again.

Colt was puzzled now. "Are you okay? Did I scare you?"

"I'm fine." Ry calmed himself. "I was just thinking that if you can't pay for the meal, maybe I could take it out in trade."

Colt laughed and said, "Anytime."

"Check!" they said together.

* * *

As they entered Ry's suite, Colt said, "After the finals, how'd you like to come up to my place and I can show you my ranch? It's only about an hour and a half north of here, just outside of Mesquite."

"I'd like that. I'm looking at some land up that way. I hear it's up and growing."

"How'd you get into land investments, anyway?"

"Well, I didn't want to be in banking. That was Dad's forte, even though that's what he wanted for me. And a friend of mine from college was looking to buy some land in Florida–Naples, actually. So, I looked at the area and I just had a feeling that he was right. My chart—horoscope that is—indicated land investing might be the way to go. I'd never gotten anything about land or real estate before from it, so I bought up a lot of land cheap and... boom. The area became the next real-estate hot spot. After that, I just always went with my gut and my horoscope, and it's paid off, literally. It drives my father crazy, which is good. Really though, I love my father. I think he might be Ophiucus—that's the thirteenth zodiac sign that's been discovered, which might explain why he doesn't understand me totally. It overlaps with Sagittarius. I'll tell you about it sometime if you're interested. I'm sorry. I'm rambling about astrology again. Anyway, to get back to my father, I just want him to understand me and be happy for me. Mom is great and she tries to help him with me."

"Parents are important. If you love 'em, show 'em. And never stop tellin' 'em you love 'em. 'Cuz you never know when you won't have 'em." Ry heard the huskiness enter Colt's voice as he said this. Colt cleared his throat. "I know you keep mentioning that horoscope stuff. I don't know a lot about it. I mean, I look at my horoscope in the papers, when I have time to read them, and they're kinda fun, but I get the feeling you're really into it."

Ry looked hard at Colt. "I am. Now this might scare you off, but I have this talent... gift... something... for reading and interpreting my horoscope. Not anybody else's—at least I don't think so. I haven't really tried.—but my own. I base all my actions around them. My investments, my appointments, my trips... my dates. I know this has got to sound crazy to you, but it's worked for me so far." He swallowed. "That's why I met you... finally."

Colt gave a slow smile. "Then how can I argue with that. Although, I am a little hesitant about something that would direct you to a dumb lug like me. I know you're successful and smart, and if it works for you, how can I argue. Maybe you could tell me more about it. I like to learn, and if it means so much to you, I want to be a part of it."

"Thank you, Colt. You're pretty smart for a big, dumb, tall, clumsy, hot, sexy, rodeo god. He put his arms around Colt's waist and hugged him.

Colt nestled his head in his hair. "Dumb and clumsy, eh?"

"I was kidding."

"What about the rest?"

"I plead the Fifth."

Colt tipped Ry's head up to his and slowly lowered his mouth to cover Ry's in a possessive, heart-stopping kiss.

Ry was totally sober now, but suddenly felt more drunk than he ever had been in his life. It was magic. There were no other words to describe it. All time and space were transformed into this one glorious moment.

With their lips still locked together, Colt swept an arm under Ry's backside and carried him to the bedroom. It should have felt awkward to Ry, but it didn't. It felt wonderful and... right.

Ry lay on the bed and Colt began to remove his jacket. "Wait. Let me do it."

Ry helped Colt take off his jacket and slowly began to unbutton his shirt. With every area of flesh that was revealed, Ry covered it with his lips. When he reached Colt's waist, the big cowboy shivered.

"This is pure agony. I think I've died and gone to heaven." He clutched Ry's head to his stomach.

Through muffled kisses, Ry managed to get out, "Not... even... close." He unzipped the straining trousers. "I've had the man. Now, I get to saddle the horse, my big Sagittarian."

Colt let out a moan, or it could have been a whinny, as Ry's mouth enclosed him.

* * *

Ry was getting more and more tense as Colt drove the jeep over the desert terrain. Colt couldn't hide his feelings about the asshole who wanted to put up a casino near his property.

"Why here. This land is so perfect the way it is! The wildlife has less and less land to live on as it is! There are enough goddamn casinos. Go down to Vegas. That's what it's there for." Colt put his hand on Ry's thigh. "I'm sorry, Ry. It's just that— have you ever seen real live mustangs? Just runnin' free and wild? They're an amazing sight. You know what? I'm gonna show you. I know a secret canyon they usually hang out in." He held out an arm. "Come here. I wanna feel you next to me."

Ry sidled into the hollow of Colt's arm and breathed in the musky scent of him. He immediately calmed and knew he could somehow work things out. His horoscope had told him today would be difficult and he had to have patience. He took in another deep breath of Colt. Patience. Common sense. Colt.

"That's my ranch off to the left. But we'll come back to it. I wanna show you the mustangs first."

They drove a couple of more miles through a small mountain pass and Colt stopped the car. "It's just a few yards up over that ridge. Come on."

They walked up the ridge and through a narrow passageway that opened into a small valley.

And there they were.

There must have been forty or fifty of them, running and darting, stopping, then running hard again, almost as if it were choreographed. Ry stared in awe. They were magnificent. He looked up at Colt.

Colt was transfixed. It was as if he was running with them. Ry could feel the excitement pouring from him. Colt was half horse. He was magnificent.

And how could he ever tell Colt.

How could he ever tell Colt that he was the asshole who'd bought the land for the casino? Colt would be devastated. But he had to tell him.

"They're incredible," Ry whispered.

"You're incredible," Colt whispered back into his ear.

"I have to tell you something, but please, listen to me first before you say anything."

"I'll always listen to you, my sweet little cowboy." Colt nuzzled his neck.

"I hope so. This is very difficult for me to say."

Colt froze in his nuzzling and straightened. "Just say it. It can't be that bad. I'm sure we can work it out."

* * *

Colt had already prepared himself for all the problems and differences between them. He knew they lived in different cities, were from different worlds really. But, he thought, they loved each other. Even if neither of them had said it, he felt it. He knew it. He loved this man and he would do anything, move anywhere, be anything Ry wanted him to be. Because whatever Ry wanted, he wanted. He never thought he could feel like this or even have the chance to have the love his parents had had. Well, he had it now and he aimed to keep it!

"I'm the asshole that owns the land by your ranch."

His ranch.

His ranch.

"No shit." Colt tried to laugh. It fell short.

"I'm going to talk to my broker. I don't think the deal is finalized with the casino people. I'm sure I can work it out or buy them out or... something."

Colt nodded. "Yeah, I'm sure you can. Money talks, right? And you've got plenty of that. And it doesn't matter anyway. I'd been thinking of selling the ranch. My rodeo days are numbered. I'm in my thirties. Bones are more brittle. They start to break. After all, if I can't pay the mortgage how am I gonna keep the ranch?" Colt knew he was blathering. Yes, he had been trying to figure out what to do after his rodeoing days were over. And he had thought about selling. But the ranch had meant so much to his folks. And to him. He loved to travel, but he loved his home, too. He'd thought of maybe raising and training some mustangs or training some of the horses for the rich folk that patronized the rodeo circuit. He'd even thought of a future with Ry. Ry had the moneyed connections. And maybe the two of them could've run the ranch and raised the horses together. "Pipe dreams", his dad always said whenever he'd talked about raising mustangs. "Ya do what ya do till you can't, then ya do somethin' else." His dad was always practical. His mom, though, had always told him to go for what you want. "And if you want it enough, you'll get it."

He wanted Ry.

"I have to go back to Boston tomorrow. This may take some time to work out, but I swear to you I'll try my best."

"I know you will, honey. And if it doesn't work out, well, then it wasn't meant to be. We'll just move on from there."

* * *

Ry's eyes misted at the endearment. How he loved this man. But this was Colt's ranch. His home. Somehow he would fix this. He would move heaven and earth for this man. He could never live with himself knowing that he had let down the most important person in his life.

"Now, how about we go back to my ranch," Colt said, putting his arm around Ry. "I'll show you around. We forget all about this... little dilemma for a while. I show you my bedroom, and I take you to heaven for a few hours. If you're going to be gone for a while, I need to give you something to remember me by—something you'll never forget, so's you'll come back to me sooner."

"You seem pretty sure of yourself." Ry snuggled into him.

"Yup."

* * *

It had taken a year. A solid year. But Ry had managed to work it out. And now here he was sitting in the same seats watching the rodeo finals and his "rodeo king" was about to make his final ride. They had talked on the phone constantly over the past year and had tried to get together, but either Ry had been too busy or Colt had been off riding in some rodeo somewhere. Even with Ry's having access to his private plane, they couldn't make it work. He'd tried a couple of times to meet at Colt's rodeos, but he'd had plane malfunctions and last minute meeting changes. It was almost as if the fates or his horoscope were working against him. His chart had told him to be patient and that time was needed in order for everything to work out right. He trusted it. He had to. But it was killing him. Every time he heard Colt's voice on the phone, he wanted to jump on a plane and be with him. Then doubts would settle in, like that Colt had been making excuses for not being able to meet him, or, even worse, had been trying to let him down gently.

But Ry was here now to see Colt and had just signed the final papers the day before here in Nevada. The Gaming Commission and land authorities had made it all a nightmare for him. But it would be worth it to see the look on Colt's face... at least he hoped so. He hadn't told Colt he would be there because he wasn't sure if he would make it in time... or if Colt still wanted him. He had to. He just had to.

"Well, well, well."

"Well."

Jed and Bo.

"We thought it had to be you. You're all Colt's talked about for the past year. You'd better have good news and a weddin' ring or Bo and I are gonna kick your ass so hard you'll think you've been ridin' a bull for a month! I'm Jed, by the by." He proffered a hand.

"Bo," the other man said. "And a simple gold band's all he'll need, but it better be eighteen karat, 'cuz we know you can afford it. And we gotta watch out for our Colt."

Ry shook the men's hands. "It's a pleasure. It's good news. It's eighteen karat. And I'm scared as shit."

Bo laughed. "Don't be. Our L'il Abner is done smitten with his Daisy Mae. He'd wait till time ended for you. You musta bewitched him or somethin.' This has been his best year ever. He's set all sorts a records."

"I know. I've been following him closely. He's amazing. And you two have just made me the happiest man on the planet. I thought after all this time... maybe... you know he'd lost interest in me... found somebody else. He's been kind of distant lately. I..." He choked up. "I love him so much."

Bo put his arms around him. "There, there, money boy. You don't have to worry."

"Bo. Must you?" Jed punched Bo's arm.

"I was just tryin' to help. And that hurt."

"Good. So, what're your plans, Ry? Ry's okay, ain't it? That's all Colt ever calls you. An' since we're gonna be family an' all."

"That's fine, Jed." Ry sniffed. "I hope so. He loves the two of you."

"Well, he sure is in love with you. You shoulda seen what he did to this really gorgeous guy the other night when he tried to hit on Colt. He—"

"Ow! Jed, why'd—"

"Don't you ever know when to shut up, Bo?"

"No."

"Then you're gonna keep on gettin' hit. I'm sorry, Ry. It was nothing. And the guy wasn't that gorgeous."

"Yes, he was."

"Bo. I mean it!"

"Sorry, Ry. Jed's right. He wasn't that gorgeous." Bo paused and looked at Jed. "'Course, I wouldna thrown him outta bed fer eatin' crackers!"

Ry was laughing hard now and the tears were streaming down his face. "You're just like Colt described. And I think I love you both already."

"Well, the feelin's the same. We feel as if we know you already." Jed grasped Ry's shoulder.

"Yeah, intimately," Bo suggested.

"Bo." Jed's warning was vehement.

"Hey, it's not my fault if Colt wanted to share the juicy details with us."

Ry felt himself redden.

"It wasn't that graphic," Jed reassured.

"Yes, it was."

"Bo!" Jed screamed this time, and the people around them stared.

"Guys, it's all right. If he feels comfortable enough to tell you, then it's all right by me." He paused. "Did he mention size?"

"Big," Bo volunteered.

"That's all right then," Ry said, trying to play along.

"But we could tell that from the way your jeans fit you." Bo's eyes ventured to Ry's crotch.

"I hope you're prepared for a lifetime of this. Bo is incorrigible."

"I'm looking forward to it." But he shifted his hands between his legs.

"Aw, you're spoilin' the view. I–"

"They're goes Colt!" Jed yelled.

* * *

Colt sprang from the gate. He had a good grip on the bronco and he felt himself ease into to the rhythm of the short ride. He knew he was on. He felt himself being watched by the masses as they screamed his name and cheered him on.

Then suddenly he felt another presence. Another pair of eyes watching him.

He was here.

Colt eyes scanned the stands, to the familiar spot where his love had watched him from exactly one year ago.

There. No. That was Jed. And Bo. And... There he was. Standing tall and beaming as he waved his black hat and cheered him on. He could ride forever now. He had come. His future. His life. His love. He was soaring. He was flying.

He hit the ground and there was blackness.

* * *

Three heads bowed. Faces wet with tears. Bo turned his head into Jed's shoulder and began to sob anew.

"Bo, come on, let's get some coffee or some food. You haven't eaten in almost a day. Ry you need to eat, too. It won't do you any good if you're too weak to tell Colt the good news when he wakes up."

"I know. Just give me a few more minutes. Bring me something back."

"Ry," Jed paused. "He's gonna make it. The doctor said he should come around. It's not a coma or nothin'. He just rattled some brains around. Colt's fallen off horses more times than I can count. He just hit the ground a little harder this time. But he's tough. He'll be fine. It was just his head." He tried to smile. "He loves you. He'll fight for that."

Ry sobbed, "Thanks, Jed. But I still feel like it's my fault. If he hadn't waved to me when he saw me, he wouldn't have lost his focus. Why didn't he jump off? He was way over eight seconds."

"He wanted to impress you. You know him. He's a show off. And he wanted to show off for the man he loves. It's Colt, Ry. Just keep the faith."

The boys left the room and now it was just the two of them.

Ry grasped Colt's hand. The tears began to flow. "Colt, please listen to me. I need you. I love you so much. You've done so much for me. Given me so much. My dad... my dad... he helped me... with you... with the deal. He called in some favors... for me. For me. He gets it now, Colt. He knows how much you mean to me. He showed me how much I mean to him. He does love me. He just wants me to be happy. He was just afraid for me. For the road I chose, you know, being gay. It's not as easy as being straight. But he gets it now. I told him. It's a lot easier if the people you love support you and love you no matter what. And you know what? He got it, Colt. He got it. And it's all thanks to you. If I hadn't fallen in love with you and become so passionate about the way I feel about you, I don't know if he ever would have understood. But he does, Colt. He does. And I want to tell you what I did and what happened between my dad and me. He cried, Colt. Dad cried and put his arms around me and we hugged and both cried. Colt, please, I need to tell you this. There's so much I want to tell you." He was crying openly now. The tears were endless. His heart was breaking.

"Colt? You know your ranch? Well, all the casino land is yours–if you want it. You just have to sign the papers, and it's yours. Mustangs, llamas, yaks, whatever you want to raise. It's yours. Please come back to me. Please. We have so much to do, so much to plan. Besides, I've retired. I have nothing to do. Nowhere to go. Nowhere to live. I thought maybe you'd let me live at your place for a while. I'm pretty good with horses, or at least I could learn. You've shown me what I want to do with my life. I'm not aimless anymore. But you've got to come back to help me. I can't run the ranch without you." He sobbed harder now, so hard he actually thought he would never stop. "And... and... my horoscope told me everything would be all right if I just followed my instincts and my heart. My heart. I have. It's never wrong, Colt. I told you. Never."

Colt's hand was covered in tears. His face, unmoving.

"My dad." Ry wiped his swiped his nose. "My dad really wants to meet you. He and Mom are flying here right now just to meet you. The man I love. Oh, Colt. I love you so much. They're gonna love you. Hey, look. I just said 'gonna.' Look what you've done to me." He half laughed, half sobbed. "I'm gonna be a shit kickin' cowboy yet! But you've got to help me. Colt, we've got so much to do and see and experience together. We're gonna have a love just like your mother and father's. You'll see. We'll make them proud. Okay? Colt, okay?" He clutched Colt's hand to his face, as if his life depended on it. And it did.

"Okay."

Ry gasped. "Colt?"

"My little cowboy. Are you cryin'?"

"Oh, Colt." New tears sprang afresh.

"Your daddy's comin'?"

"Yes. Yes."

"Your mama, too?"

"Yes. Colt, I thought... I thought you–"

"Were gonna die? Are you crazy?" He coughed. "When the man of my dreams, the love of my life, my entire future is waiting for me? I guess you do think I'm a dumb, big, tall, sexy, hot, perfect, Adonis, Hercul–"

* * *

His mouth was covered in a kiss that would keep him going and thriving for decades. His pain forgotten, he savored and enjoyed the taste and kiss of the man who made him complete.

A sob came from the doorway. Bo rushed to the bed.

"I knew you wouldn't die!"

"Bo, please! Do you have to be so morbid. I knew you were tough, Colt. And you also had a big reason to stick around." Jed sniffed and hugged Colt harder than he meant to.

"A big reason. Boys, I guess you know this is my future, right here in my arms. We've got a lot more land and we're gonna have mustangs and llamas and yaks–"

"Hey, how much of my sob story did you hear?" Ry demanded.

"I think I came in right after your dad helped you with the deal."

"You heard all that?"

"Yup."

"Then, I guess you heard me say 'I love you.'"

"Yup."

"And do you have anything to say to me?" Ry looked at Colt.

"Yup."

"Say it!" Bo yelled.

"I love you, Ry. With all my heart and soul. I've loved you from the moment I set eyes on that fantastic little backside–and that not so little front side. From the moment when you hit me with that little half-smile and I saw those deep blue eyes, I melted and I was yours. For now and always."

The emotion in the room was palpable. Jed spoke up. "Don't you have something to give to him, Ry?"

Ry reached into his pants pocket. He pulled out a piece of paper. "This is our horoscope for today... and the future."

"What—" Bo started.

Jed glared at him. "Hush, Bo."

"I have a confession, my little—not so little—Sagittarian. I've been reading my horoscope and studying about astrology for a year now. Every damn day."

"I'll be dipped–"

Bo received a sharp elbow in the ribs from Jed.

"You did that for me?" Ry's eyes started to mist.

"If you believed in it, I knew there must be some truth in it." Colt paused and grabbed Ry's hand. "Because I believe in you."

"Thank you, Colt," Ry choked out. "That means more than you'll ever know."

"Shit," Bo mumbled and wiped at his eyes.

"I hope you're learning something here, Bo," Jed said and took his hand.

"I guess I don't need to read this then." Ry started to fold the paper.

"I want to read it." Bo snatched the paper from Ry and began to read through his sniffles. "When two Sagittarians come together they form a unique bond that other signs can't touch. They do all they can to please their lovers and satiate their common interests and desires. They are true to one another and have a bond that others envy. It is a near perfect relationship." Bo shoved the paper into Jed's chest. "Aw shit. I'm gonna cry again." Now he buried his face in Jed's shoulder.

"It's okay, baby. I think you're near-perfect too." Jed rubbed Bo's shoulder.

"You do?" Bo raised his head to look at Jed.

"Uh huh. Near perfect. You could still use a few lessons. Maybe try reading your horoscope once in a while. It seems to work for them."

Ry reached into his pocket again. "Colton James, I want to spend my life with you. Will you spend your life with me?" Ry displayed an exquisite plain gold band before Colt.

"You wanna marry me, little cowboy?"

"In the worst way, my Rodeo God."

"Rodeo God. I moved up from Rodeo King?" Colt said.

"Rodeo God?" Bo gave a disgusted looked.

"Shut... up, Bo." Ry, Colt, and Jed said together.

Colt looked up to the ceiling. "Mom, Dad, whaddya' think? Is this the guy?"

The lights in the room flashed.

Everyone but Colt gasped.

"I guess that means yes." Ry kissed him hard, and Bo and Jed embraced.

"Holy shit," Bo uttered. "Jed, you and me need to start reading our horoscopes starting yesterday–so we can catch up. I wanna know what it says about all of this."

Ry looked up. "Thank you for giving me your son. I will do my best to love him. Thank you for your blessing."

Colt added, "Thanks, Mom and Dad for believing in me. This is the man, and this is my future and my happiness. Ry and I will do you proud."

The lights flashed a final time.

CAPRICORN

The Goat

Traits: Practical, Prudent, Ambitious, Disciplined, Careful, Humorous, Determined, Fatalistic, Miserly.

Gardner Braxton stepped out of the way to avoid a three-hundred-pound woman as she tried to maneuver her way through the narrow corridor of the Great Pyramid of Khufu.

"Excuse me," the enormous woman said. "I can't believe they don't have better access in these places. Do you know who I should complain to, young man?" The woman had stopped moving, while Gardner kept himself pressed against the wall, the rough brick scraping his back. Thankfully, he'd been holding his camera bag/backpack, or there wouldn't have been enough room.

"Haven't a clue. Maybe the tour guide?"

"Yes, I'll start with him. And you should cut your hair. You have a very handsome face. Nice square jaw. It's a shame to hide it. And..." The woman moved in closer and peered at him. "... yellow-green eyes. How interesting. A lovely contrast with the sun-bleaching in your honey-colored hair—which is too long, I might add." The woman turned away and continued her waddling.

"I haven't had time to cut it, maybe later." Gardner hadn't cut his "honey-colored" hair in a couple of months and it was getting a little unruly. He had to keep pushing the locks off his forehead. Besides, it was too hot for the climate. And what was with the intense assessment of his looks?

Tourists, Gardner thought. Where would all of the great sights and exhibits of the world be without them? Maybe I will cut my hair today. It'll be cooler. He brushed back a lock and some sweat along with it. He was trying to get some good photos for the book on the Seven Ancient Wonders of The World that his editor had been expecting six months ago. Even though it wasn't his fault, the book was late. He was always on deadline, and usually early. He'd come to a snag with this book, though. He was going to try to reconstruct the other six Wonders (since the others had all been destroyed) through the extant bits and pieces, and then use the wonders of modern technology. But he'd been doubting this plan for a while now. It seemed like cheating. All of his other travel/history books had been actual photos, the good thing being, they'd actually sold—and quite well, affording him the opportunity to travel to his heart's content, whether he was working on a book or not. Although, all the places he'd traveled to seemed to wind up in some book or other. There were just so many great and amazing places to see—a hell of a lot better than all the war zones he'd been in in his former life. War correspondent. Yuck. What had he been thinking?

He'd been thinking of all the good he wished he could do with his photos and articles. In point of fact, he had helped—or so people said. But there was definitely a burn-out point. He'd achieved it two years before he'd stopped. But he'd just kept plodding along. Then Kevin had come into the picture. One phone call and his life changed.

"My name is Kevin Franco, and I've admired your work for years. Have you ever thought about writing a book? I'm the Senior Editor at..."

And the rest was history. Thank you, Kevin. He owed him. Big time. He'd probably saved his life. So... he needed to get this book done. And he'd tried. Granted, he'd traveled to the sites of the Wonders, but only the sites. He was going to—for lack of a better word—Photoshop them in at the original sites. But he needed something special for this. A gimmick. He'd figure out something. He always did. He just wished something would come to him soon.

He thought he'd at least get some good—authentic—pyramid photos, and he would send them to Kevin, along with the accompanying narrative. But even this was not going as planned. The pyramid had been closed for some construction reason or other. Hadn't the pyramids already been constructed? What? Were they renovating? Cleaning?

He pushed away from the wall, watching the last vestiges of flowered dress go around a corner up ahead. He thought he'd made sure he was the last of the line of tourists, so he could take his time photographing. He didn't know how he'd missed the woman.

He felt something in the wall. A loose brick? Maybe that's what the construction was about? He wiggled the brick. It moved. He pulled a little harder. It came free. He looked around. Everyone was up ahead, not too far; he could still hear voices.

He reached into the crevice, hoping this wasn't one of those "Indiana Jones" traps and his hand wouldn't be severed.

Something was in there. He withdrew his hand and pulled forth an object.

A gravy boat? No. It looks like Aladdin's lamp. Give me a break. This must be here for tourists to find. But how would a tourist find it? He'd only stumbled on it because he was pressed up against the wall. It was beautiful, if a little dusty. How do I get it out of here? He picked up Canon camera bag, unzipped it, and looked in. His $2000, 50-500mm telephoto lens stared at him. If I took that out, there might be room. Yeah. I'll just attach it to the camera. No one'll know what the lens is for, or that I couldn't possibly use it in here—I hope. Just what I need, get caught stealing some Egyptian relic from a 4000-year-old tomb. He knew the Egyptians did not look kindly on that sort of thing, and their punishments could be severe. Like cutting off my hand. Kevin Franco, his boss would love it. I don't care. I'm taking it. It's worth the risk. He maneuvered the lamp into his bag. It fit perfectly. Like it was made for it. He affixed the lens to his camera and moved on.

The rest of the tour seemed interminable, and Gardner was sure someone was going to question why he wasn't taking any pictures.

They had just entered the King's Chamber—the largest of the chambers—thirty-four feet high and nineteen feet wide. All the walls were pink granite, and the sarcophagus at the center was red granite. It had no lid and stood in the center of the chamber. It was quite large. Gardner couldn't remember the exact dimensions from his research, but it was big. He also noticed the possible ventilation shafts at the north and the south of the chamber. The southern one pointed toward the belt of Orion—or where it would have been in that time—in the night sky. The northern shaft pointed to the circumpolar stars. It was thought these shafts could help guide the spirit of the dead pharaoh to find the important stars. The Egyptians and their beliefs. Whew. But they did manage to build these incredible structures. Maybe their Gods did help them. Or someone. Or something. He was jostled from his thoughts.

"Young man," the fat woman again. Where had she come from? He hadn't seen her in an hour. And there she was, right next to him. "You've been lugging around that camera all afternoon and haven't taken one picture. Don't you know how to use it?"

"Uh, yes," was his insipid response.

"Well then, take a picture of me in front of that coffin-thingy. The red and pink should look marvelous with my dress." The woman waddled over to the sarcophagus. "And take off that lens. You can't use that in here."

Gardner was stunned for a moment. How had she known? He took off the lens, not knowing what else to do.

"I'll give you my e-mail and you can send it to me." The woman tugged her dress into place, then adjusted her breasts. "There. How do I look?"

Hideous. "Great. The orange and yellow in your dress goes great with the red and... pink."

"Thank you. I knew it would. You do know how to use e-mail don't you?" The woman fluffed her flouncy, dark brown hair a bit.

"I've done it a few times before. Now, smile. I'll take a couple of pictures."

"Wait. Is this a good angle? I don't want to look fat." The woman adjusted to the right a little.

"Don't worry," Gardner said, trying not to choke. "You look great." He snapped the photos.

"All right then, here's my card with my e-mail. If you have problems, you can just have copies made and send them to me. My address is on the card as well." The woman shoved a card at him.

"No problem. I'll get right on it," he said.

"I should hope so. What other type of lens are you carrying there in your bag? Something else you can't use? Let me see." The woman reached for his bag.

Gardner panicked. "It's... another telephoto... it's broken... I forgot I brought it." He yanked the bag out of her reach.

"Well, why don't you get rid of it? It must be heavy. Then you could put the other one in there." The woman pointed a pudgy finger at the camera case.

"I will when I get back to the hotel. There's no place to throw it away here." He made a sweeping gesture of the chamber. "We should probably catch up to the group. I haven't seen them for a while."

"If you'd been paying attention, you would have heard Abdullah, or Mohammed or whatever his name was, say that the tour ends here and we are free to leave anytime now. And now that I have my souvenir photos—and you had better send them soon, young man—we can go."

This woman is impossible. "Sure, as soon as we get back, I'll send them." He proffered a guiding hand. "After you."

After another hour, Gardner finally found himself back in his small, but serviceable, room. He'd had to get a suite to ensure a toilet and shower—no tub, but a decent sized shower. He didn't really mind spending the money; he wasn't parsimonious—he was frugal. All those years of struggling, trying to make it as a photojournalist, were still with him. He used the toilet, but the shower could wait. He was the only one there and didn't mind his own smell, although the mustiness from the pyramid seemed to linger on him as well. He took his shirt off. That feels better anyway.

He sat on the bed with his camera bag and opened it. Is it still there? Unzipped it. Yep. He gently removed the lamp from its snug, secreted spot. He held it up to the light by the handle. "Is it gold? They used to use that all the time. If it is, it's got to be valuable." He went into the bathroom and got a hand towel. Maybe if I remove the dust and dirt I can tell better. He rubbed the lamp. The grit came off easily. It is a desert. Sand everywhere. The lamp seemed to get warm. He felt his fingers tingling. The lamp was magnificent. All gold. Solid gold. No wonder it was heavier than it looked. A gravy boat for a pharaoh. Gardner chuckled at his gaffe, and said aloud, "But if it's not a gravy boat, what is it?"

There was a knock at the door.

Surprised, Gardner almost dropped the lamp. "Who is it?" He furiously stuffed the lamp back in his bag.

No answer. "I'll be right there." Gardner put the bag on the floor on the other side of the bed, away from the door. "Coming."

He opened the door.

There stood the most beautiful man Gardner had ever seen. Shirtless. White linen, baggy—almost harem-like pants—cinched at the waist. If ever there were a V-shaped body, this guy had it. Huge shoulders, broad chest—hairless—tapered waist. His skin was completely bronzed. It actually looks like it's painted. The skin was flawless. And his face... flawless. Squared, strong features, an aquiline nose, jet-black, wavy hair curling at the nape—and electric-blue eyes. There's no other way to describe them. Gardner half expected lightning to issue forth from them. The man's arms were crossed over his chest, making his pectorals bulge even more. Taut nipples peeked just above his crossed forearms. His biceps also bulged with veins running along the topside of each. Incredibly sexy.

"You called?" the husky, dark voice said.

For the first time in his life, Gardner understood what dry mouth was. There was not a drop of spittle to be had. That's when he realized his mouth had been agape ever since he'd opened the door. He closed his mouth and tried to swallow, wiggling his tongue along the roof. He had to say something. What was he supposed to answer? He didn't remember calling anyone. Was he room service? He snorted a laugh. Like this guy could be room service. Which made Gardner start thinking of the "services" he could provide as well as the "services" Gardner would like to provide in return. "Come in," he finally managed to say.

The man stepped into the room. *What am I doing? This guy could rape and kill me with one hand tied behind his back. Whoa. Where'd the rape thought come from?* He'd just invited a perfect stranger into his room. Emphasis on perfect. In spite of his size, although they were the same height, six feet or so, this guy had more muscle. The man didn't seem to be threatening. *Yeah, neither did Ted Bundy or the Boston Strangler.* "I don't think I called you." He was hoping he had, though.

"You summoned me."

Summoned? It is Egypt. "Um, and what did I summon you for? You'll have to refresh my memory. I was out all day in this God-awful heat. Maybe it got to me."

"Whatever you desire."

Gardner gulped. "You're kidding, right? I know I didn't order a male escort. I'd certainly remember that—heat or no heat. But if I did, you'd definitely be my choice. Shit. Sorry, it just slipped out. I didn't mean to say that." He couldn't resist adding, "Out loud."

The man quirked a corner of his mouth.

I amused him anyway.

"Feel free to express your thoughts and desires." A dark look came over his face. "I have heard much more over the years." The man looked away, as if remembering.

"I bet," Gardner said. "Anyway, thanks for not making me feel too awkward. I'm Gardner... or Gard, whatever, but really, why are you here?"

"I will call you whatever, you wish."

"Gardner, then. And I wish you would tell me how you got here, since I didn't call you, and why you are here."

"The lamp. And... for you," the man answered succinctly. "One."

"One?" Then the realization struck Gardner. "The lamp! You know about it? No, it's not possible. It's an Arabian Night's tale." He shook his head in denial. "Are you trying to tell me I found Aladdin's lamp—rubbed it—and here you are? A genie? Get out. I'm not that naïve. Did Kevin put you up to this? That prick. Just because my book's a little late..."

"I do not know this Kevin. And I am not a "genie." That is a bastardization of my name—Djinn."

"Djinn, genie, it's all the same. It's a load of crap."

"I have heard this many times before. Your saying it does not stop its truth." Djinn finally unfolded his arms.

Gardner gave a short intake of breath at all that flesh being bared before him. "And if you're a... Djinn, why do you look like that? You're everybody's idea of perfection," he said, not caring now what came out of his mouth. He was too pissed off.

"I am your idea of perfection. That is why I appear as I do. It is part of my tasking, to appear as the lamp bearer wishes me to

appear. You are pleased, are you not?" Djinn smiled, knowingly.
"Might I add, that you are also a very fine looking man."

Gardner pulled back. Was that a flirt? He said aloud, "Are
you flirting with me? Are you gay?"

"If you are saying, do I prefer men, the answer is, yes. But I
have been with women as the occasion has arisen," Djinn said with
some distaste.

"I take it that didn't work out?" Gardner noted Djinn's
reserve.

"I do what is wished of me," Djinn said, closing the
conversation.

Knowing Djinn was gay, and that he thought Gardner was
good-looking, changed Gardner's thoughts. Maybe I'll let him hang
around for a while. He's certainly great to look at. All that naked
muscled flesh. Yeah, I couldn't have chosen better. "So what
happens now?"

There was a knock at the door.

"Now who? King Tut? Coming," he called.

Gardner opened the door onto a mass of flowers.

"Did you send me my pictures, young man? Where's your
shirt?" The woman from the tomb shoved past him into the room.
"Oh my!" She stared at Djinn. "I'm so sorry. I didn't mean to
interrupt..." She came further into the room. "Who is this? Is this
your boyfriend?"

Gardner felt himself turn crimson. "I... I..."

"Yes, I am," Djinn said, proffering a hand. "I'm Djinn."

It was the woman's turn to blush. She took the hand, coyly saying, "I'm Petulia—named after that 1960s movie with Julie Christie. Veeee-ry nice to meet you."

Slightly recovered, Gardner said, "I'm Gardner, by the way. Braxton."

Petulia turned to him. "I know. I recognized you right away at the pyramid, from all your wonderful travel books. I have them all. I thought maybe you were incognito and didn't want the rest of the group to know. But even your scraggly hair couldn't hide that beautiful face from me. And now I see you have a beautiful body to go with it."

Gardner felt himself redden again, noticing how his tiny room was with the three of them in it. He wanted to cover himself. "Thank you."

"Oh please, it was nothing. And why didn't you bring your boyfriend to the pyramids?" Petulia turned to Djinn again.

"I was there," Djinn said, smiling at her.

"You couldn't possibly have been," Petulia said. "I certainly would have noticed you."

"I was hiding, trying to keep away from the crowds." Now Djinn smiled at Gardner and winked.

"I know. Tourists. They're just impossible, aren't they? So, Gardner, I'm surmising that you've been a little busy here..." She looked from him to Djinn, the implication obvious. "So, if you'll let me know when my pictures are ready... I'm in room nineteen."

"You're staying here?" was Gardner's vacuous reply. "I didn't realize. I wish I had them ready for you now. But I'll..." He looked over at the bed. Petulia's gaze followed his.

"Two," Djinn said.

"Oh you dear, dear boy! She brushed by Djinn and went to the bed, reaching down. "They're beautiful."

Gardner was speechless. How?

"When did you find time to get actual photos made?" She turned coyly to him, all of her pushiness evaporated. "Would you do me one little favor?" Petulia cocked her head coyly. "Would you sign them for me?"

This woman is delightful. She just totally charmed me. "It would be my pleasure," Gardner found himself saying.

"Here." Petulia reached into her more ample bosom and withdrew a Sharpie. "Always prepared."

Gardner and Djinn both laughed. Djinn said, "Delightful."

"Isn't she?" Gardner averred. "For the most beautiful woman in Egypt..." he said as he signed, leaning on the small bureau next to the door.

"Oh." Petulia's eyes misted. "I can't thank you enough. That's the sweetest thing anyone's ever said to me."

"Here you are, Petulia." Djinn handed her a handkerchief. "And I must say, I agree with him. You are the most beautiful woman in Egypt."

Petulia started to sob. "Oh my... you boys... you're the nicest couple I've ever met. You've made this the best trip I've ever had."

She blew her nose into Djinn's handkerchief and sniffed. I was so alone and feeling blue, and now you two—"

Finished writing, Gardner said, "Would you like to join us for dinner?"

Petulia abruptly stopped sniffling. "Oh, I couldn't. You boys need your time together. You don't need a fat old woman—"

"Please," Djinn said. "We could think of no more charming dinner companion than yourself. Seven o'clock? In the lobby? I know a wonderful restaurant."

"I wish you would, really," Gardner reassured.

"Three," Djinn whispered. Gardner jerked his head at him.

"If you insist... I would love to." Petulia walked to the door, entranced.

"Your photos." Gardner handed them to her.

"Oh yes, thank you. Thank you so much... for everything. Seven, then. In the lobby." She closed the door.

Even with Petulia gone, the room didn't feel any bigger. Djinn emanated presence—and sex. "I think I should shower. We've got an hour or so," Gardner said. He couldn't possibly spend an hour getting ready. What was he going to do the rest of the time? His dormant libido and mind had some suggestions, but he needed to ignore them.

"Wouldn't you like to ask me some questions, Gardner? You seem nervous. I am not going to hurt you." Djinn sat on the bed. "Please sit with me."

Gardner silently moved to the bed and sat. The air grew heavy and thick with sexual tension. Only a foot or so separated them.

Finally, Gardner ventured, "How did you make those photos appear?"

"You wished for them."

"Right." Then Gardner remembered, "You said 'three' right before they appeared. And you said 'one' and 'two' earlier..."

"Wishes."

"But I say, 'I wish' all the time. Everyone does."

"I noticed you do that. You really need to choose your words more carefully, Gardner. The phrase, "Be careful what you wish for," is several thousand years old. I would know." Djinn gave a wry smile.

"You're several thousand years old? This is too much." Gardner stood up, then turned to Djinn. "If that was my third wish, then I'm done? No more? I wasted them? I mean... this is ridiculous. There aren't wishes. You're not a genie or Djinn or whatever."

"Gardner, please sit."

Gardner reluctantly sat. The momentary tension forgotten with the thought of genies and wishes.

Djinn began didactically, "The truth about having three wishes has been altered over the centuries. In actuality, the wishes are limitless. But... after the third wish, the Djinn has the judgment to grant the wishes in the manner in which he deems appropriate. I am sure you have heard many a tale about wishing to be able to touch something and turn it into gold, or the like. Most of the tales are true.

The people who made these wishes were driven by power and greed. As a Djinn, I chose to end their reigns of terror."

"So you're a good Djinn?" Gardner was trying to make some sense of this.

Djinn laughed. "Not particularly. I have no designation in that regard. I do, however, make judgments when one of my owners harms another individual. That is when I use my discretion."

"Like who? Anyone I've heard of?" Gardner was giving Djinn leeway, although he couldn't have said why.

"Most of my owners," Djinn answered. "Several have been very prominent in history."

Gardner looked a question.

"Very well. I am sure you are acquainted with a rather short Frenchman, who discovered the lamp on his tour through Egypt."

"Napoleon?"

"The same."

"What did he wish for that you stopped him?"

"He wished to have enough troops to battle on two fronts in England and Russia. Unfortunately, his ego, which was rather larger than anything else about him, got in his way. I gave him the troops, but, in his power-mad mind, he neglected to wish for victory. Well, let me say, it escalated from there. Every wish had consequences. He wished to be invincible. He was. Personally, only. He became so frustrated, he was afraid to talk... or wish. He was tormented. He relinquished the power of the lamp and ended his days on St. Helena—a broken man."

"Who else?" Gardner was intrigued now.

"Alexander, I believe you refer to him as The Great."

"That's right. He was in Egypt on his conquering campaign. I'm guessing same deal with conquering dreams."

"Yes."

"But his lover, Hephaestion, who was killed, didn't Alexander wish him to live?"

"Indeed he did. But even I do not have the power over life and death. I am not almighty."

"I see." Gardner nodded, then said, "At least as much as I can. I need to think about this. I wish..."

"Be careful, Gardner."

"Right. My head is spinning with all this. I'd say I need more proof, but how many times can I wish for something just to convince myself. I mean, you did those photos for Petulia. That should have been impossible. But you did it." Gardner stood abruptly. "Petulia. I need to get cleaned up. I guess you can use the shower after if you'd like. Or do you, like, automatically clean up?"

Djinn smiled. "I can, as you say, automatically clean up."

"Nice trick. Are you going to wear a shirt or something? I mean, you're practically naked." The elephant appeared in the room again. Gardner felt himself redden as he stared at Djinn's naked torso.

"I will dress appropriately." A smile again, this time more than friendly.

Gardner went to the bathroom. The hot water felt wonderful on Gardner's body. The small bathroom steamed up quickly. He tried to clear his mind and enjoy the cleansing water, but found his thoughts filled with the handsome Djinn only a few feet away on the other side of the door. He felt himself getting hard. "Not good," he muttered. "It's been way too long." He soaped himself and found his thoughts now filled with Djinn. And the fantasies began. He imagined Djinn with him and lost in his thoughts uttered, "I wish this was your hand Djinn."

Gardner felt a body pressed to his back. Another hand had a firm grasp on him. He felt the exquisite pleasure of the stroking. The slick body rubbing him from behind. He was lost in the sensation, not really sure, or really caring, if this was real or his fantasy. He only knew he didn't want it to end. The steam completely engulfed the shower; he sucked in the moisture-filled air. He breathed harder and harder as he approached his climax. The slick, muscled flesh against his back heightened the sensation. He felt his orgasm building. The strong masculine hand forced him along, making him a prisoner to his need.

The incredible eruption came; his body transported in bliss. It went on and on. No thought. Only feeling. Flesh against flesh. Hard stroking.

Gardner slowly became aware again, his breathing still labored. He was alone. Did that just happen? That was amazing. He rinsed and shut off the water. His body still tingled from the orgasm.

He quickly toweled off and wrapped the Egyptian cotton towel around his waist. He reached for the doorknob, anxious to see if Djinn was still there. He paused, now feeling embarrassed. If Djinn had really been there in the shower with him, this was going to be awkward. And if he wasn't... it would still be awkward. Oh well, I can't stay in here forever.

He opened the door. Djinn was seated on the bed, exactly where he'd been before, except now he was dressed in a short-sleeved, white cotton shirt, white trousers, and flat brown sandals. He was devastating, his tanned skin a perfect complement to the stark white of the fabric. But it was the eyes Gardner noticed the most. They bore into him, almost searing him with their intensity and sexual desire.

It was real. Djinn had been in the shower with him. Instead of feeling awkward, Gardner now felt desire burning within himself. He gazed intently back, lost in those vivid eyes, not noticing or caring as the towel fell from his hips.

Djinn's eyes lowered and he slowly said, "We have to meet Petulia in five minutes."

It was a cold bucket of water as the realization of the words sifted into his brain. "What? Oh right."

"There will be time later."

The subtext could not have been more obvious... or more exciting to Gardner.

"Is that what you are wearing? I am sure Petulia would not mind, and I highly approve." Djinn said, staring boldly at Gardner's arousal.

Gardner followed Djinn's eyes to his waist, drew in a quick breath and scrabbled on the floor for the towel. He hadn't realized he'd gotten hard again.

Gardner held the towel to his waist and shuffled by Djinn to the closet door, brushing Djinn's shoulder along the way with his exposed rear. "Excuse me."

"No need."

Gardner grabbed a pair of light khaki slacks, eschewing underwear—as he would have had to go back to the other side of the room to the dresser to get them—slipped on some sandals, and donned a light, cerulean blue, button-down shirt. He buttoned a couple of the bottom buttons and declared, "Let's go meet the lovely Petulia."

"You look very handsome, Gardner. I hope Miss Petulia won't be too distracted."

"Not with you there. I'll just fade into the wicker-work."

Djinn opened the door. "After you."

* * *

"So after my husband died, ten years ago, I've been traveling and seeing the world. I'd hoped to find someone new to share the rest of my life with, but I seem to have been at cross-purposes. For, while I've been traveling the world, I've also been eating around the world. At almost sixty years old and three hundred pounds, I'm afraid no man would want me." Petulia took a forkful of her kushari, Egypt's national dish. As she munched her lentils and chickpeas, a look of self-pity momentarily crossed her face. Gardner had a twinge of pity for the woman seated across from him.

"This restaurant is wonderful, Djinn. However did you find it? The taxi driver must have made at least twenty turns getting here." Petulia took another forkful.

"It is a favorite of the local people—and a favorite of mine as well.

Authentic in every aspect," Djinn responded. "You are enjoying it, Gardner?" He reached out and covered Gardner's hand with his.

Gardner had just scooped up some ful medames on the wondrous Egyptian bread. He bit in and tasted the garlic and lemon with the fava beans. Delicious. And so was the heat from Djinn's hand. "Very much," he answered, almost coyly.

"You two boys make the most gorgeous couple. It makes me happy to see the two of you so obviously in love." Petulia dabbed the cloth napkin to her eyes.

Gardner pulled his hand from Djinn's. "Uh, Petulia, we—"

"—are very thankful," Djinn finished.

Gardner stood. "Uh, where..."

"Behind us, through those curtains," Djinn finished once again.

Gardner made his way around the small, round, wooden tables, which were placed so close together he wondered how the waiters could maneuver, but they seemed to with no problem. The restaurant was small, but every table was occupied. They were the only non-Egyptians, he noted. Is Djinn Egyptian? He doesn't really appear to be. He speaks it perfectly, though. Thank God, or we would've starved. The waiter doesn't speak English. He pushed through the beaded curtain and noticed a wooden door immediately, and as this was the only door, he opened it. Yep, this is it. Not bad. At least it has a flushing handle. And a sink. He turned on the spigot and splashed cold water on his face. He held the sides of the sink and closed his eyes. What is happening to me? A Djinn? Love? What did Djinn think? A quickie in the shower, and it was time for hearts and flowers?

Although, Gardner found himself admitting, it had been a pretty spectacular quickie, and if he were to be in love with someone, Djinn was the perfect specimen. But he's a genie, sorry—Djinn. "This is so out of control," he said to the wall. "What am I going to do? I guess I could wish him away. Shit! But I don't want to. Not yet. Gardner, Gardner, Gardner. Just go with it. He's sweet. He's blazing hot. And he has magic. What's the downside? None. Yet. Okay. I'm gonna go for it." He turned and walked out of the bathroom, resolved with his decision, and returned to the table.

"Feel better?" Petulia asked.

"Remarkably so," he said. Gardner grabbed Djinn's hand this time. "What's for dessert?"

Djinn eyed him with a peculiar stare. "Konafah, of course."

"Oh, what is that?" Petulia piped in.

"Actually, its origin is very mysterious. You can find it in ancient medieval Arab cookbooks, as well as Turkish ones. Its actual origin is unknown. It is made by taking a noodle-like pastry and, while it is in its liquid state, it is drizzled onto a hot plate until it hardens. Then it is mixed with butter and wrapped around a filling made of nuts or whipped cream—or both. I prefer both." Djinn looked hotly at Gardner. "Do you?"

Gardner's mouth was dry again. He could only nod and stare back.

"That has to be the most sensuous description of a dessert I've ever heard," Petulia said. "You two should take some back to the room and eat it off one another's bodies."

Both men's mouths dropped open and they stared at her.

"I was married for almost thirty years." Petulia gave a half-smile. "I may not look it now, but I had my day, and I learned a thing or two."

Both men began to laugh, tension broken.

Gardner said, after wiping the tears from his eyes, "You are the most enjoyable woman I have ever met. You embody the word delightful."

"Thank you, Gardner," Petulia said, somewhat demurely. "You've both made me very happy. It's been a while." She dabbed at her eyes. "Now for some konafah! Extra whipped cream, please, Djinn."

"Your wish is my command." Djinn signaled to the waiter and gave a knowing look to Gardner.

* * *

So, Gardner, my dear, I know you must have a wonderful project you're working on. Can you give me some insider details? I'm sure it's going to be fabulous." Petulia leaned into Gardner as she scooped the last dollop of whipped cream into her mouth. "And, Djinn, thank you so much for this incredible meal. This konafah was to die for. And if I eat anymore I will die. You've ruined my diet." The men stared at her. "I'm joking with you boys. I would love to lose weight, but I love food too much. I'm afraid I'm hopeless. So tell me about your book, Gardner."

Gardner sighed. "I have to confess, my plan was to do a travelogue of the Seven Ancient Wonders of The World, but I've come to a standstill. I've visited all the sites, but that's all they are—sites. No structures. I thought I would be inspired by the areas and do a time-travelish, romantic cruise through the ancient world. And the areas are beautiful—don't get me wrong—but I don't know how to recreate the Wonders without being cheesy."

"That sounds like a wonderful idea! I would buy it in a second. The text will be as beautiful as your photographs. You are so talented. Why don't you just use your imagination to transport the reader there? Make it romantic. You have Djinn here for inspiration." Petulia paused. "I have an idea—if I might be so bold?"

"Please, Petulia, I'm open for suggestions. I'm already six months overdue on my deadline," Gardner said.

"All right. It is the 2000s and everyone is becoming so open. And that darling Anderson Cooper came out, and there were no repercussions... why don't you use your and Djinn's romance to take us to these wonderful sites. Tell us about how romantic the places are, seen through the eyes of two lovers." Petulia looked from one man to the other. "You would both certainly be eye candy for the book." She smiled and winked.

Gardner felt himself blushing.

Djinn, who had remained silent, now spoke up. "Petulia, my dear, I believe that is a wonderful idea. We will revisit the sites and Gardner will become inspired. I have some expert knowledge on the Wonders, which I believe will help." He looked at Gardner with a knowing smile.

You probably saw them being built, Gardner thought, but said, "Thank you, Petulia. That's a great idea." It would be a good idea if, one: it was possible, two: if Djinn wasn't a... Djinn, and, three: if I was in love with him. He mused, then said again, "Yeah, a great idea."

"I'm glad you like it," Petulia bubbled. "I guess we should be getting back. I'm sure you boys have something better planned tonight than spending time with me." She smiled again, her insinuation so obvious that Gardner felt the heat in his face rising once again.

"We love your company, Petulia, perhaps a nightcap back at the hotel?" Djinn offered.

"Thank you, but no. I want to go to the bazaar tomorrow, so I need my beauty rest." Petulia giggled.

"Very well," Djinn said. "Shall we depart?"

* * *

They returned to the hotel, after wishing Petulia a final goodnight.

Djinn closed the door to their room. Gardner sat on the bed and stared at him. "Thank you for a wonderful evening, Djinn. You were very charming. Petulia loves you." He started to feel claustrophobic. The big man stood at the door, seeming to dominate the room—and Gardner's thoughts.

"Thank you, Gardner. You were also quite charming. I sensed a reluctance on your part with Petulia's suggestion for your book. What are your doubts?"

Besides the big, three-letter-elephant-in-the-room: S-E-X? He had to say it. "You're a Djinn and we're not... lovers... and..."

"Do you want to be?"

Gardner stared at Djinn, trying to think of a response. Yes. No. Maybe... Yes.

Djinn moved toward him. He reached out and took Gardner's hand and pulled him up to him... then kissed him.

Their lips melted together. Magic. Gardner's arms instantly came up and surrounded Djinn. He opened his mouth and the kiss deepened. He felt the hardness of Djinn's body with his hands, a sharp sensual contrast to the softness of his lips and mouth.

The kiss continued for several minutes, until Djinn slowly withdrew, saying, "What do you wish, Gardner?"

Gardner instantly pulled away—the magic gone. "I can't. The wishes. Is that all this is? You're kissing me is because I have that stupid lamp... and it's what I wish? I don't want you to be in my power because of that." He made a vague pointing gesture to the closet where the lamp was hidden.

Djinn's voice was calm, as he said, Gardner, "I am not kissing you because I am under the influence of your wishes or because you have the lamp. I am kissing you because I desire you."

Gardner once again found himself staring at Djinn. "Oh."

"I would also like to help you with your book. Did you like Petulia's idea?"

Gardener reluctantly said, "Yes, but the photos are still a problem, and we're not—"

"Lovers," Djinn finished. "Would you like to be?"

Gardener couldn't deny it. "Yes."

"Very well. I would also like that very much," Djinn said matter-of-factly, but with an underscoring of sensuality. "I am also able to help with your photographs. You have used your three unconditional wishes, but as I told you, you may have more. I am able to transport you wherever you wish."

Gardner cocked his head at the thought. "Can you travel through time?"

"Of course."

Gardner's head started to spin at the possibilities. "You mean we could travel to the actual sites and see the Wonders? Live?"

"Yes."

"It's that easy? I would like to see the Wonders, I think, right before they were destroyed. It would give them a weathered look, as opposed to looking new. It would give my book more veracity." Gardner shook his head. "As if anyone would believe it." Gardner hesitated. "But what about the 'wish' consequences?"

"Gardner, as long as you are not hurting anyone, your wish is my command."

Gardner started to laugh. Then laughed some more. He was out of control and fell back on the bed in hysterics.

"Gardner, are you all right," genuine concern in Djinn's voice. He went to the bed and sat, holding Gardner by the shoulders, as the paroxysms of laughter rocked through Gardner.

A couple of minutes later, Gardner composed himself, and still in Djinn's arms said, "You actually said..." He paused to contain another outburst. "Your wish is my command!" He began to laugh again.

Djinn turned Gardner to him and stifled Gardner's laughter with a smoldering kiss.

Gardner instantly responded, laughter forgotten.

A moment later, Gardner pulled away and whispered, "I have an idea... and a wish, I guess."

"Please, tell me."

Gardner gave him a delicate kiss and said into Djinn's mouth. "I wish we could make love in the King's Chamber in the Great Pyramid of Khufu."

Djinn's eyes grew dark. He smiled slowly, sensuously. "Would you like to bring your camera?"

"Good idea." Gardner started to breathe heavier in anticipation.

"I have many good ideas," Djinn said. "Let us go."

"What about lighting? It'll be dark."

"All taken care of," Djinn assured.

And it was. The King's Chamber was somehow, dimly—but romantically, Gardner thought—lit. Magic can be pretty useful. The stone floor of the chamber was hard against Gardner's back, as Djinn pressed him into the floor, his full weight upon him. "Maybe this wasn't such a great idea," he said, wresting his mouth from Djinn's. "I wish we had some padding." Gardner instantly felt soft cushions beneath him. "Wow. I could get used to this wishing thing."

"I am glad you are enjoying it," Djinn said. "Anything else you wish?"

"Yes. I wish... you would show me your many good ideas."

"I will be happy to grant your wish." Djinn's mouth descended.

In spite of the coolness of the chamber, Gardner felt the heat from Djinn's body even through his clothing. He wanted to touch that hot flesh. He'd wanted to ever since Djinn had appeared half-naked at his hotel room door.

As if sensing Gardner's desire, Djinn quickly divested Gardner of his shirt and then tossed his own aside.

Djinn, ever so slowly, lowered himself onto Gardner. As each inch of flesh made contact, a hot brand was scorched there, making Gardner suck in his breath from the rush of feeling.

Gardner had never before felt this desire for anyone. He had had only a couple of relationships, and those were long distance and unfulfilling. He'd never had the time or inclination to pursue them. Even sex in various parts of the world he'd traveled was sporadic— not that he didn't like it. It just seemed as if it was never a priority. At this moment, however, with Djinn, his mind and body raged for sex. His only priority.

Djinn's mouth covered his; their tongues met and teased, taunted, dared. Gardner's hands plied and kneaded Djinn's muscular back and shoulders, relishing the strength and texture of the taut muscles.

Djinn flipped Gardner over and began to perform the same erotic massage on Gardner's own back. Every touch and movement made Gardner want to cry out with pleasure. He should be a masseuse for a living. He'd make a fortune. I guess after four thousand years, he's honed his skill. The thought prompted a momentary pang of jealousy—a new emotion—for him. He wanted Djinn all to himself. Always.

Djinn's hands moved around to the front to Gardner's waist, and he adroitly unfastened Gardener's pants and slid them off. Their lower bodies met. Djinn was naked. Magic again. Man, is it ever! Gardner wriggled against him feeling the large erection bantering with his own. An incendiary desire to see all of Djinn, overtook him. He flung Djinn over and abruptly stood. And stared. Oh my effing God. There's perfection... and then there's... Djinn. How could someone look like this? Every part of him is burnished and chiseled. No Greek, Roman, or Egyptian god could even come close to comparing.

And then he looked to Djinn's eyes. They mirrored his own. The appreciation and desire were equal. Gardner knew he was passable in the looks department, but from the look on Djinn's face, he felt impossibly desirable to him. "You're..."

"Beautiful," Djinn finished.

Gardner's desire, somehow, incredibly grew. He drew his eyes to the inviting juncture between Djinn's legs. Djinn spread his legs slightly and Gardner knelt before him. He needed to taste him, to take him in. He'd never felt such a compulsion. He lowered his head.

Djinn's groan in response was all Gardner needed. He was out of control. Teasing. Licking. Stroking. He continued, until in a violent movement, Djinn wrenched himself away from Gardner and said, "I wish to return the favor, before I am undone by you. There is much I still wish to indulge with you."

"The words heated Gardner like nothing he'd ever experienced. He laid back, staring into Djinn's eyes, waiting, begging... wishing for the returned 'favor.'

His wish was granted and Gardner found himself lost in pleasure. Time was suspended. He felt himself getting ever closer to climax. Then as the final build began, a thought intruded into his mind. Is this only incredible because Djinn's using some magical technique? It's not real then, is it? Djinn said he wanted him, but did he really? Was this magic sex? Gardner abruptly stopped Djinn's ministrations.

"Djinn," Gardener panted. "I have to know something. Are you using magic to make this all so great?"

Djinn's eyes rose from between Gardner's legs to meet him. "I am hoping you are thinking this is magical."

Gardner stared into the dark orbs. "That's not what I mean. I mean, yes, this is magical, but are you using magic to make it so?" He felt a little embarrassed now as he voiced his concern, especially with Djinn's head between his legs.

"No, Gardner, I am not using magic." Djinn sounded hurt. "Would you like me to stop?"

"No," was Gardener's immediate response. "I... I only meant... Ahh." Too late. Djinn went back to the task at hand.

Over the next several minutes, Gardner had managed to maneuver himself so that they were both able to give each other satisfaction. Their simultaneous releases only made the climax more intense for Gardner. He hoped Djinn felt the same.

"I have never experienced that with anyone, Gardner. Thank you for sharing it with me." Djinn's eyes stared the length of Gardner's body until they met his own.

Gardner felt a rush of warmth, even as their slick bodies parted. The coolness of the chamber did nothing to quell the feeling. He turned himself around and propped on one elbow, caressed the side of Djinn's face with his free hand. He peered into Djinn's eyes and received a look of intensity that Gardner had never seen in his life: love. Gardner sucked in his breath. He was afraid. *I need to protect myself. This is a fantasy. A great one. But I can't fall in love with him. Yeah, how do I do that? I think I already have.*

Djinn, seeming to sense Gardner's reticence said, "Gardner, let fate decide."

Gardner was confused, on many levels. "Fate?"

"Yes, fate or destiny or whatever you believe. I have experienced all religions and beliefs. We determine our own destinies. Even I and my creator will at some point have to choose for ourselves.

"Creator?"

"Yes, there is another like myself. I will tell you about him at some point in the future. But for now, I believe you have a book to research. Do you have enough information and inspiration for the Great Pyramid?"

Gardner picked up to the, not so subtle, "inspiration" reference to their love-making. He leaned down and firmly kissed Djinn. When he finished, he pulled back slightly to see that both their ardors had been inspired again. He reached down and grasped Djinn strongly in his hand. A small groan escaped Djinn's lips. Gardner said, "This inspires me to say, I wish see the Colossus of Rhodes." He squeezed hard. "I want to see how you compare."

Djinn groaned again. "I hope you will not be disappointed." A final squeeze.

"I'm sure I won't be."

Djinn smiled. "The giant bronzed phallus it is."

It was dusk. The sun was setting over the crystal blue of the Mediterranean, where it met the Aegean, on the isle of Rhodes.

"Incredible," Gardner said in awe as he looked at the horizon.

"I agree with you," Djinn said looking at Gardner.

Gardner turned to look at Djinn looking at him. "I meant the view."

"As did I."

Gardner gulped. "Thank you." He looked past Djinn's shoulder. "Is that a trireme?"

Djinn followed his gaze to the ship that was passing by them. "Close. It's the smaller, faster version, the liburnian. They were used mostly for war, and I believe this era is peaceful."

"What year is it?"

"226 B.C., days before the earthquake that will destroy this magnificent statue." Djinn swept his arm up behind him.

Gardener's gaze followed the movement.

There it was right behind them. Towering. The Colossus of Rhodes. They'd been standing in front of it.

Gardener's jaw fell open. "Oh-my-God!"

"Helios, actually. God of the sun," Djinn rejoined.

"This is unbelievable. It so huge. I... Shit. I wish I had my book about the Wonders."

Gardner looked down to his hand. There it was.

"Is this the book you meant?"

Gardner chuckled. "That's it. Thank you." He flipped open the book. "The Colossus stands 110 feet high without the pedestal, which is 50 feet. And... ah hah! He's holding the cloak. It's not draped over a shoulder as many assumed. And he wears a crown, and his right hand seems to be shielding his face from the sun. Ironic, don't you think, as he's the Sun god and all."

Djinn chuckled. "I could have told you these things, but I see you are much more pleased to have discovered them for yourself."

Gardner was noticing the people around him, for the most part dressed in traditional toga-like garb. "Uh, why is nobody staring at us? Look how we're dressed." He displayed the shirt and pants they had worn since dinner with Petulia.

"They cannot see us. I have made it so. Would you like a different form of dress?"

"No, this is fine. That's pretty cool." Gardner stared up at the Colossus. "He is naked. And big." He stared at Djinn, feeling desire come over him. "Is it a selfish wish if I wish to make love with you on the pedestal between his legs?"

Djinn's eyes darkened. "Yes. But you would not be hurting anyone... at least I hope not too much."

"Then that is my wish," Gardener said.

"Mine also."

They were naked. Magic could be convenient. Gardner stared up at Djinn standing over him in a pose mimicking the Colossus.

"The pose is the same. Same musculature—big. His skin is darker—bronze will do that. And he's a little stiff. But not as stiff as you are." Gardner eyed Djinn's engorgement. "And he is bigger, by several yards, I'd say. But not as accessible." He reached up and grabbed the body part in question and pulled Djinn down to him. Djinn groaned.

"You're sure no one can see us?" Gardener said.

"Do you want them to?"

"No. But it does give an added thrill being out in the open like this. Even if they can't see us, I still feel like an exhibitionist. I've never done this." He squeezed Djinn, eliciting another groan from the man.

"Nor I, Gardner. As you appear to have a solid grasp of the situation..." He joined his hand to Gardner's and gently removed it. "And since you seem so fascinated with the Colossus..." He stepped back several feet.

Gardner's jaw fell open as he watched Djinn grow and expand. He continued to grow until he became the same height as the Colossus. They were almost identical, the largest difference being Djinn's now enormous erection. Djinn mimicked the Colossus' pose.

Gardner stared, overwhelmed. Djinn smiled and waved from on high.

Djinn remained that way a few moments longer before returning to his normal size—erection intact. "Are you through with your comparison?" Djinn gave a wry smile.

"You were the model for the Colossus of Rhodes?" Gardener gaped in astonishment.

Djinn cocked an eyebrow. "I didn't want you to wish that you were with him instead of me."

Gardner paused at the statement. Was Djinn jealous? Could I really have had that wish come true?

Djinn answered his thought. "Yes, you could have wished to be with him."

Gardner lightened the growing serious mood. "I like my men big, but that's a little ridiculous." He laughed and reached for Djinn. "This seems perfect to me."

Djinn's eyes darkened and suddenly Gardner felt himself rising into the air. He gasped. His grip on Djinn grew stronger.

Djinn chuckled with a sexy warmth and pulled Gardner to him.

"No magic carpet?"

"Not for what I intend." Djinn kissed Gardner as they rose.

A sudden soft bump on Gardner's head broke the kiss. "Ow." Gardner raised a hand and rubbed his head as he looked up. He had just bumped his head on another "head." That of the penis of the Colossus of Rhodes. "Very funny."

Djinn laughed heartily. "I only wanted to reaffirm that if you had considered wishing to be with him, your wish might not have turned out as expected."

"Ah yes, the twisted genie wish." Gardner rubbed his head again, realizing they were several stories in the air having casual bantering. "Don't you have something else to show me?"

"Indeed." Djinn slowly descended Gardner's body, his tongue tracing every curve and muscle of his torso. He trailed to Gardner's feet, then began a slow ascent. He paused midway and said, "This is only for you Gardner. I want you to remember this forever."

Gardner sensed an underlying meaning, but replied. "How could I not?"

Their eyes held a moment before Djinn enveloped him and Gardner became lost in sensation.

The sun had set. The waters churned in the sea. They lay in each other's arms, enjoying the smell of the sea and each other. They were on level ground now, on the pedestal supporting the statue, which still loomed directly above them. The pillows—courtesy of Djinn—provided comfort from the marble-covered wood.

"Where would you like to travel to next?" Djinn whispered as he nuzzled Gardner's ear.

Gardner thought a moment, distracted by the nuzzling. "I wish... you to surprise me."

"Ah, Gardner, I warned you, be careful..."

Gardner put his hand over Djinn's mouth. "I trust you."

A look of tender warmth came into Djinn's eyes. "Thank you." He pulled Gardner to his feet and encircled him in his arms. "Close your eyes."

Gardner eyes were closed and he held the muscular Djinn tightly to him. He instantly felt the climate change. The air was dry and he could smell water, but not from the sea. He felt Djinn pull away from him.

"Open your eyes."

Gardner did. Completely surrounding him were tiered walls of incredible flowers and plants.

The Hanging Gardens of Babylon.

It appeared to be early morning. The sun had barely risen and was casting a golden aura over the walls and into the courtyard where they now stood. There didn't seem to be anyone around.

Gardner took in the brick terraces and columns all around, noting the large gaps in the terraces to allow room for some truly magnificent trees to flourish. He breathed in. A variety of scents from the multitude of flowers assaulted his nostrils.

"The smells are incredible. This is amazing. No words could ever do this justice. Did Nebuchadnezzar really build this for his wife because she was homesick?" Gardner asked.

"Indeed he did. Her land was very green and mountainous. He created this mountain and the Gardens all for her." Djinn paused, looking at Gardner. "He loved her very much."

The air became still. Gardner nodded slowly. "He must have. She was very lucky." Gardner looked away, fearing he'd betrayed his

132

feelings. I can't fall in love with him. He's a Djinn. He's immortal. This can't go anywhere. Except, I don't know how to stop myself. I've never met anyone I ever felt this kind of attraction to. He's amazing... and not just the Djinn part... the man himself. So kind and... loving.

"Is everything all right with you, Gardner?"

Gardner was pulled from his reverie. "Yes, I'm just overwhelmed. Walk with me?" He held out his hand to take Djinn's, then pulled back. Better not get too close. I need to protect myself. Gardner paused occasionally to take pictures, of course, but for the rest they just enjoyed each other's company.

They came to a set of stairs. "What's up there?" Gardner asked.

"I am not certain. I have seen these places before, but you must remember, I was rarely given the opportunity to experience anything for my own amusement."

Gardner's thoughts turned inward. I'm an insensitive clod. He's been a slave his whole life. He's never had the chance to really experience anything on his own. And he's still a slave... to me. The thought sickened him. "May I ask you something?"

They paused on the stairs. Djinn turned to him. "Of course."

"How did you become a Djinn?"

Djinn gave a melancholic smile. "I was taken from my village, which no longer exists, south of Baghdad. I was chosen by the Grand Djinn to be his companion and protégé. I have never known why he chose me, nor does it matter. I was thirteen. For twenty years I was his student and servant, little knowing that I was being groomed to take his place in the lamp."

"But where did he come from? Why is he a Djinn? Where does his magic come from?"

Djinn laughed. "So many questions. To which I have no answers. Grand Djinn would not ever tell me and would punish me harshly when I tried to press him."

Gardner sensed he had touched a nerve and changed the subject. "So the Gardens don't really hang, they kind of droop and spill over the walls. How do they water everything? Wait." He reached in his pack and pulled out his book. "It says that they used a chain-type system to lift the water high into the air from the Euphrates. That's pretty advanced, I'd say."

"The Babylonians were very innovative in many ways, Gardner." He looked intensely into Gardner's eyes.

Gardner suddenly had the urge to kiss him. He pulled Djinn close and their mouths met. Tongues thrashed together. "Make love to me," Gardner said, pulling his mouth away an inch from Djinn's.

"Is that a wish?"

"It's whatever it needs to be. But can we go up on top of that wall up there? I want to take in the view of all this magnificence." Gardner said, then added, "And I kind of like this outdoor, exhibitionist kind of thing."

"As do I."

The next thing Gardner knew, they were atop the highest terrace looking down at the sumptuous gardens, with the Euphrates on the outside. "I can see the water pulleys. Amazing. The men there must have to monitor it twenty-four-seven. It's seems to be constantly moving. But I guess with miles of flora to irrigate you'd have to." Clutched in Djinn's arms, Gardner felt a sense of belonging. They stood on top of the wall and surveyed the splendor of it all.

Gardner felt a nuzzling on his neck, and Djinn's tongue began to trace along from ear to shoulder. That's when Gardner realized they were both naked. How did I miss that little maneuver? Or Djinn's obvious erection pressed into my butt? Then he had a thought. Standing up could be interesting. Another first for me. He wriggled and adjusted his rear into Djinn.

Djinn complied and adjusted as well.

"Please..." Gardner said. He felt pressure... then exquisite pleasure.

They both moaned and began their motions toward fulfillment.

When they had finished, they both sank down, their knees unable to hold them erect any longer, both replete and satisfied, Gardener still enfolded in Djinn's arms.

"Amazing," Gardner said.

"Yes. Amazing. Where would you like to travel next?" was Djinn's rejoinder.

"The Lighthouse?"

Gardner saw Djinn's face flatten. "Not the Temple or the Tomb?" Djinn quickly asked.

Gardner didn't want to destroy the mood, sensing something wrong here, so just as quickly he said, "How about we check out the other statue? I don't suppose you were the model for that one, too?"

"I never said I was the model for the Colossus, as for Zeus, he's so much older looking, Djinn said. "Let me show you."

It appeared to be mid-afternoon and they stood before another magnificent edifice. Gardner smelled sea air as he took in the area surrounding them, trees and mountains everywhere, man-made flattened areas far off to left. For the Olympic Games? "I thought the Parthenon was beautiful. Of course, I guess all the buildings look better when they are newer. When are we?"

"168 B.C., two years before the first earthquake causes much damage here," Djinn informed.

"Guide book." It appeared in Gardner's hands. As he flipped through pages, he said, "I know this is the one Wonder they're not exactly sure of what happened. Ah." He stopped flipping and read, "Built around 432 B.C.—it's certainly holding up well—in the style of the Parthenon and the Temple of Diana, which we get to see later. Right?"

Djinn nodded.

"And... blah, blah, blah... he stopped. The Statue is in the west section of the temple. Ready? Hey wait... Why am I wearing a toga?" He just now noticed the change of dress. "And you, too?"

"When in Greece?" Djinn smiled. "I thought you would be more comfortable and assimilate better to the period."

"And there's no underwear?" Gardner gave a flip to the lower portion of his toga.

"Not invented yet." Djinn smiled again, with a hint of a leer.

"Right. It would make a few things easier, I suppose."

"It does. And I will be happy to show you."

Gardner's mind ran to prurient thoughts and he felt himself stir.

"I see the thought does not displease you." Djinn stared pointedly at Gardner's waist.

Gardner felt himself redden, although why he should be embarrassed now, he didn't know. "How did the Greeks deal with this? I guess, unless you strapped it down, or didn't have much there, everyone could see. Like now." He looked down at the tented fabric.

"Many Greeks enjoyed showing off their... wares—as you should. You have much to admire."

Gardner noticed movement now in Djinn's toga. Speaking of much to admire. "Well there's no one around. Odd. No? Any guesses where they are? A pilgrimage, a religious holiday?"

"Perhaps the latter. There are many gods to worship, and they all need their just adoration. Jealousy, you know."

"Right, those Greeks and their festivities." Gardner suspected Djinn had somehow arranged it all so they could be alone. And he appreciated it. It made his photography easier. And of course the love-making. What he didn't understand was the constant urge to be with Djinn. He thought that, physically, he wouldn't be able to perform so often. What's that old trope? "Don't look a gift horse in the mouth." That was a Greek who said it, I bet. Or a Trojan. He laughed aloud.

"Something amusing, Gardner?"

"Just remembered an old Greek proverb. Let's go see the king of the gods."

They climbed the marble—of course—steps to the pedestal, stepped between the columns, and entered the temple.

Gardner took Djinn's hand. Just two gay Greeks going to pay homage to the king of Olympus.

Djinn squeezed Gardner's hand. "I have never held hands with another man. Thank you."

A lump came to Gardner's throat. He knew the comment was innocent and heartfelt, which made it all the more tragic. Gardner squeezed back.

They only walked a short distance until Gardner could see the enormous statue looming down the corridor. The ceiling was cavernous. No cathedral had ever been more impressive. He knew it was slightly over forty feet high, as the statue of Zeus was forty. The width of the base was twenty-two feet, he remembered. The statue filled the entire area, making it seem even larger.

They stopped at Zeus's feet and stared up. Ivory and bronze had been used for the skin. The upper torso was bare. The long skirt the god wore was of gold, as was his beard. He held a golden statue of the goddess of victory, Nike, in his right hand, and a scepter of every conceivable metal of the era topped by a jewel-encrusted eagle. Even more magnificent, was the throne. Gold, ebony, ivory and every precious gem Gardner could ever think of rested beneath the god. Gardner had never felt so small and insignificant. He understood why the Greeks would come here. While the rest of the temple was almost barren, a Greek proclivity, this statue imbued power and grandeur of such an enormous scale nothing else was needed.

Gardner's camera appeared before him. "I believe you have a job to do," Djinn said in his ear.

"Right. This is incredible." He began to click. "Oh, by the way, he is too old to be you." He snapped a few more photos, backing up as he did so. "But he's still pretty hot looking."

"Perhaps you would like me to bring him to life for you?"

Gardner stopped his photographing and turned abruptly to Djinn. "You could do that?"

"If that is your wish?"

Gardner sensed the admonishment, and said, "And you would keep him forty-feet tall, and he would stand up and bring down the roof, then he would try to have sex with me with a ridiculously large, ivory and bronze, or gold, or whatever, penis."

"It's a thought."

"Keep your thought. Let me work." Gardner went back to photographing. "So, what is the real truth about how the statue was destroyed? Some said fire, some said earthquake, some said a wealthy Greek guy took it for his private collection. That would have been a logistical nightmare. Some said Constantine pillaged it for the gold—"

"It was Constantine," Djinn cut him off. "Early fourth century A.D. He had it stripped of its treasures. It was later destroyed. A fire."

"You seem certain."

"I aided him."

"You belonged to Constantine?" Gardner was still in awe of the incredible things Djinn had witnessed... and done.

"For a time."

"Another megalomaniac?"

"He became so. He tried to defeat the Persians. He did however accomplish some great feats."

Gardner felt odd pushing him too far and let the matter drop. "These shots are going to be spectacular."

"When you are finished, I have a surprise for you," Djinn called to Gardner, who had backed away down the corridor to take in the entire statue.

"Almost finished," Gardner said. "And where's my backpack? I know it doesn't go with the toga, but then, what does? A laurel wreath maybe, or those arm cuffs." He felt the tightness on his biceps and a rustling in his hair. "I didn't say I wanted them. I only meant—"

He stopped as he approached Djinn seated before Zeus's throne, a feast of foods displayed around him on a golden silk carpet, plush pillows scattered at the edges.

Djinn raised a goblet to him. "The bracelets and laurel do you justice. Here, Gardner. Ambrosia. The nectar of the gods."

Gardner took the chalice and seated himself next to Djinn. This man is amazing. I would love him even if he weren't a genie. Zeus, or someone, help me! He looked into Djinn's eyes and raised his goblet to Djinn's already upraised one. "I thought ambrosia was a myth—or a salad."

"No, Gardner, it exists. Over the centuries the concoction became altered, until it was forgotten, never to be recreated. Even in this age the mixture has been changed."

"But you know the original recipe?" Gardner held the cup to his nose and inhaled. Extraordinary.

"I see you like it. There are a few advantages to being thousands of years old."

"Wait." Gardner said. He linked his arm through Djinn's. "I've always wanted to do this with someone I... know," he lamely finished.

Their faces mere inches apart, Djinn said, "Yes, it seems a little intimate to do with a stranger." His eyes darkened. "I am glad I know you, Gardner. You are a fine man. And after we have dined and drunk our fill of ambrosia, I will get to know you better."

Gardner couldn't speak; the sexual promise obvious. He didn't need ambrosia, he had Djinn.

"Drink, Gardner, and come to understand why it is called the nectar of the gods."

Arms still linked, eyes locked together, they drank.

The thick, rich liquid caressed Gardner's tongue and throat with a soft delicacy, as if his mouth were being slowly painted. The flavor indescribable, no singular taste. It was in constant flux. Sweet, tangy, slightly sour, spicy, pungent, then slight alterations and combinations. No flavor lasting long enough to secure it. There was no flavor; there was every flavor. Every texture. To say it was intoxicating would be an egregious understatement.

Gardner's eyes closed as he savored and absorbed. Time stood still as he enjoyed. He felt his lips part as more of the exquisite liquid passed his lips, and he felt a mouth cover his own. The nectar passed between them, sharing, swallowing. Gardner felt it running down his cheeks and neck, only to be captured by hot lips. The fluid flowed onto his chest, and as it spread, a sensuous warmth emanated from wherever it touched. As Djinn lapped the nectar from his body, every nerve was stimulated from the mere touch of his tongue. Djinn pushed Gardner's toga off and poured the ambrosia onto his lower body. The liquid splashed but never flowed off, as though it had a life of its own. Djinn's mouth followed the path downward, getting every drop. Djinn's tongue wandered back and forth over his abdomen, gradually, agonizingly getting closer. Gardner sensed when Djinn reached his goal. Gardner's climax would be swift, yet transcendent. And when it came, excruciatingly slow moments later, he was not disappointed. It was exactly as it should have been—like a nova, an enormous burst, then burning itself out. But something was missing.

Gardner wanted more. The ambrosia wanted more. The experience was not meant to be for one. It was meant to be shared. By lovers. He shoved Djinn onto his back and slowly poured the liquid over the only man he wanted to share this with.

Djinn. His lover.

Djinn lay taut as a bowstring.

Waiting.

Gardner took in the glistening liquid covering Djinn.

He lowered his head and began his attack.

Afterwards, Djinn lay in Gardner's lap, enjoying the figs and dates being fed to him.

"May I ask you something, Gardner... personal?"

"You may." Gardner popped a fig into his own mouth, and with his other hand rustled Djinn's long hair.

"Do you want to have someone to share your life with? Someone to love?"

I'm treading dangerous territory here. How do I answer this? "Yes. Yes, I do."

"And you have never found anyone? You are a kind and wonderful man, Gardner."

Gardner was very glad Djinn could not see his face, for he could never hide his feelings now—not after the ambrosia. And the Gardens. And the Colossus. And the Khufu pyramid. And... He needed to answer him.

"I will be as honest as I can be. I have been with other men, a few I thought had potential but didn't work out. So I have always had my work, and I thought that would be enough to satisfy me. I thought content was good enough. I've learned recently that I was wrong. My work is not enough. I need to share it. I need to share my life. I want to share someone else's life. I don't want content. I want to be happy. And I want to share happy with someone who also wants to be happy." He shook his head in exasperation. "I think I might be that old cliché, a romantic fool. But it's what I want."

"You are not a fool, Gardner." Djinn sat up and looked seriously at Gardner, then said, "Where, or as you would say, when, would you like to go?"

Gardner tried to clear his head and make some sense out this insanity. "Halicarnassus?"

"Tomb of Mausolus it is."

And there it was before them.

Stark and white, rising 140 feet into the air. The pyramid-shaped roof comprised a third of the entire structure. The sun was setting low in the sky behind the tomb, appearing as a halo emanating behind it. Gardner gazed in awe.

"I know this building was around a lot longer than some of the other Wonders, but when are we now?" Gardner asked.

"1200 A.D., right before the first of the series of earthquakes that will eventually destroy the tomb during this century."

"Artemesia, the queen of Halicarnassus, had this built to honor her husband Mausolus, hence the term mausoleum. And he was also her brother?" Gardner paused from reading his book. "Wow. It says it was a common practice then. I thought only the European royals had that market. I guess she really loved him."

"There are many concepts, Gardner, that were accepted then, which later became taboo or thought immoral or sacrilegious. I have seen and experienced things that were never recorded in your histories."

"Anything you'd care to share?" Gardner was feeling playful... and horny again. Go figure.

Djinn smiled slyly. "I would like to share much with you. But first you must work and take your photos."

Gardner's mind whirled to thoughts of unknown sexual fantasies with Djinn as he dug out his camera. "Why don't you read me some more information about the Tomb, while I get my shots. This lighting is incredible. Talk about magic hour."

Djinn smiled once more and took the book from Gardner. "You may have noticed there are no people present. They are preparing for a siege."

"Siege?"

"Quite common here. This area of Asia Minor is a very valuable and strategic territory."

"It also gives us the chance to be alone... or almost."

"A consideration." Djinn winked.

Gardner inwardly swooned. I'm a teenager. This is not good.

"Are you hungry, Gardner?"

Food. How come he wasn't hungry? "Why am I not hungry? I love to eat. And after expending all that energy..."

"It is part of the time paradox. Sleeping, eating, become irrelevant."

Gardner began to wonder. "Do you have to eat and sleep?"

"Yes, my body requires rest and sustenance." Djinn responded. "But I can go without them for quite lengthy periods."

"Oh. Good to know." He stared at the structure, musing. An idea began to form. "You see that statue in the middle between the columns. I think it's Zeus—or maybe Apollo. Could you remove it for a couple of minutes?"

"Of course. Why? Your photo will not be authentic. It is Apollo."

Gardner hesitated. "I would like you to stand there. Naked."

Djinn slowly smiled and cocked his head to one side.

The next instant Djinn appeared as requested, naked and magnificent between the enormous marble columns. His bronzed skin made a bold contrast to the stark white of the columns. Gardner slowly mounted the steps toward him, taking in the bare musculature of the man, noting the bulging biceps of his crossed arms and the sheer power he exuded. Another idea came to him. "Would you please hold your arms up and out to the sky?"

Djinn complied. Gardner began taking a series of photos. I hope he doesn't realize I'm taking these photos for my own collection. I have to have something to remember him by." He felt his throat closing at the thought of never seeing him again. I can't lose him. I've never felt this way before. I didn't think love was a possibility for me. And it's definitely love, beyond the superficial. There's a goodness in this man. A guarded caring.

Gardner thought about the pseudo-relationships he'd had, none lasting more than a couple of months, and that was with... What was his name? He couldn't remember, but he'd thought that one might have had a chance. But there was really nothing beyond the sex there—and now after Djinn, he realized even the sex hadn't been that good. *What am I going to do? I'm going to enjoy this for as long as it lasts, and when it's over I will have my memories, photos, and my career. Who am I kidding? It all seems meaningless now without someone to share it with. Is this what I've been searching for all over the world? I guess so. And now that I've found it, I see what my life is all about. Nothing. All the money and fame amount to... nothing.*

"Gardner? Are you all right?" Djinn broke his reverie.

"I'm fine. Just planning my next shot." He sniffed and realized there were tears in his eyes. *Self-pity. So not my style.* He stared at Djinn.

Djinn stared back. Gardner noticed a change in him. A big change. Flaccid to erect. "You enjoy this?"

"I'm enjoying the anticipation of what's to come."

Gardner was within a few inches of Djinn—not close enough to touch. "You and these columns make me think of Samson. I would love to tie you up between the columns."

Djinn's eyes darkened—not with desire—but with a look of anger. "Why would you wish this, Gardner?" his voice restrained.

Gardner looked away. *It's not a wish. It's a want. I don't know what I was thinking.* Never mind I—"

"Look at me, Gardner."

Gardner looked up. Djinn's eyes had softened.

"If that is what you want..."

147

White silken cords appeared on all four of Djinn's appendages, securing him to the columns on either side. "Is this what you had in mind?"

Gardner visibly gulped. Hot could not begin to describe this. "Something like that," he mumbled.

"What else would you like?"

Gardner thought. "I would like you to be blindfolded." A white sash covered Djinn's eyes. The blindfold made it easier for his next requests. "Some scented oil... and a silk... flail."

Djinn's abdomen noticeably tightened. Gardner was glad he couldn't see his eyes.

I have to do this right. "And I want your promise that you can't and won't try to free yourself."

Djinn inclined his head to him. "You have it."

Gardner was filled with anxiety and trepidation—but most of all, lust. He looked at Djinn's feet and discovered the requested objects, as Djinn said, "Is that satisfactory?"

"I can work with it." Gardner removed his clothes. He was achingly aroused by his prurient thoughts. He stepped close to Djinn, still not quite touching, their twin arousals separating them. Gardner's thoughts began to coalesce. He reached down into the pail and slathered oil onto his hand. The oil had a vanilla and some other unidentifiable scent that was very intoxicating. He bent down and slowly applied the oil to Djinn's right foot, massaging the soles and instep, tugging the toes. Djinn sighed with pleasure. After several minutes, Gardner moved to the other foot and copied the movements, eliciting a new series of sighs from Djinn.

Now Gardner changed tactics and instead of oil-covered hands, he used his tongue to ascend Djinn's leg, moving all around, back to front, then back again, till he reached the juncture of Djinn's hard thighs. Djinn's entire upper torso tightened each time Gardner's tongue touched a sensitive area. Gardner reveled in watching the muscles flex.

He repeated the tongue laving on the other leg, then reached to the oil bucket once again. He worked the oil and his fingers up and down each leg until they were glistening.

Gardner was aching to caress and devour the most male part of Djinn but knew he must restrain. He was in as much painful want as Djinn, he was sure, but the wait would be worth it—for both of them.

Gardner moved to Djinn's hands and arms. He had his system down—tongue, hands, and oil. Gardner noted the added sensitivity in Djinn's palms and beneath his arms. Note to self.

He moved to Djinn's head, using his hands to massage Djinn's scalp, while his tongue worked on his ears an neck. Djinn vocalized his pleasure in a series of ahs.

Gardner progressed to shoulders, then back. As his mouth explored Djinn's back, he firmly kneaded the taut shoulder muscles the residual oil from his hands aiding the sensual massage, and periodically he added more. He moved lower, and kneeling, ministered to Djinn's taut buttocks, squeezing and stroking, and a new idea formed for later.

He moved to the front. Gardner stared for a moment, taking in the beautiful muscles on display. Lightly running a hand from neck to sternum, he now changed tactics. He splayed both hands over Djinn's chest and began to massage. He moved over Djinn's upper body, pausing occasionally to lick or nibble a hardened nipple to educe a throaty gasp from Djinn. The taste of the oil was surprisingly delicious, as if it were made for consumption. Knowing Djinn, that was the intent.

Gardner had never done or even fantasized about the things he was doing with Djinn right now, and was pleased that Djinn had not spoken one word, just let him play out his fantasy. He wanted Djinn only to experience and enjoy.

Oil to the chest and more massaging... and finally downward. Gardner applied a gentler technique, not wanting an ending. He could sense Djinn's mounting need as his cries became more insistent.

But there was more to come.

After using hands and mouth to bring Djinn to the edge several times, he stopped.

Gardner went to the bucket and began scooping oil out and applying it to his front. As he did so, he listened to the pants issuing from Djinn, enjoying the pleasure he had given him. Gardner finished oiling and moved behind Djinn.

Body contact.

Gardner pressed his full body to Djinn's; every inch of the front of his body connected to Djinn's backside. Gardner's hands slid around and encompassed Djinn's chest, pressing them impossibly closer. Gardner moved his face in Djinn's hair as he slid his body back and forth. He moved his hands lower on Djinn and began to squeeze, stroke and fondle. Djinn moved with the motions, causing ripples of sensations in Gardner.

Gardner felt himself firmly nestled between Djinn's buttocks and now began to ever so slightly adjust himself. He felt a subtle stiffening in Djinn's body and Gardner sensed was something was wrong.

Djinn's momentary slight was gone and he began to move with Gardner again. Gardner continued to rub over Djinn for several more minutes until he felt his own climax mounting. He stopped. He moved away from Djinn and went for the as yet unused flail. It lay next to the bucket, white, a riding crop-like handle with several tendrils of silken fabric attached.

Djinn, still silent but for the panting, waited.

Gardner picked up the flail and stood before Djinn. He slowly draped it over Djinn's genitals and began to make circles. Djinn's body unconsciously moved with the motions.

Gardner pulled away and flicked Djinn's right thigh. Djinn gasped. Gardner bent and kissed the spot, slowly moving his lips over the stung area.

"Ahh." Djinn rocked his head back and forth.

SNAP. The left thigh. Then a sensuous kiss.

SNAP. Right pectoral. Kiss.

SNAP. Left pectoral. Kiss.

Gardner trailed the flail over Djinn's lower abdomen and around to his back.

SNAP. Left shoulder blade. Kiss.

SNAP. Right shoulder blade. Kiss.

Gardner pressed his body up against Djinn's once again and whispered as he licked Djinn's ear, "More?"

Djinn nodded slowly.

SNAP. Left thigh. Kiss.

SNAP. Right thigh. Kiss.

Gardner found himself not enjoying the act of the whipping so much as the obvious sensual pleasure he was giving to Djinn. That was the turn on—giving pleasure.

SNAP. Left buttock. Kiss.

SNAP. Right buttock. Kiss. But this time Gardner lingered, explored. He reached between Djinn's legs and fondled.

A couple of more minutes of this and Gardner knew they were both ready. More than ready. He moved around to Djinn's front and remained there a short while, enjoying these last tense moments, leading to the culmination.

Gardner slid up Djinn's body and closed his mouth over Djinn's. This first kiss was all they both needed. As the kiss deepened, their oil-slicked bodies moved in unison over one another's.

The kiss became frantic and both men felt the pressure build.

Gardner ripped away the blindfold and beheld the most wondrous look from Djinn as their eyes met and they climaxed together.

Afterwards, they lay on the marble steps, Gardner sitting between Djinn's legs, while he held him to his chest.

Gardner spoke, "I wanted you to trust me."

"I do."

Djinn turned Gardner's head around. Their eyes met. "Thank you," Djinn said, then lowered his head and softly kissed him.

Gardner opened his eyes, staring into Djinn's. He sensed something different. "I don't think we're in Halicarnassus anymore."

Djinn smiled at him. "No, Dorothy, Ephesus. Welcome to the Temple of Artemis."

Gardner turned around and once again gazed in awe. "Would you like me to read," Djinn offered, bringing forth Gardner's book. They were still clad in togas.

"I know some information about this. I saw the extant remains in the British Museum, along with some marble from Mausolus's tomb." Gardner said. I know this is the third and largest of the temples to Artemis created on this spot and that it was destroyed by the Goths in two—"

"Sixty-eight A.D." Djinn finished. Four hundred twenty-five feet long by two hundred twenty-five feet wide."

"It is enormous. And so many columns." Gardner reached for his backpack, which was, of course, not there.

Djinn handed him his camera.

"Thank you." Gardner removed the lens cap.

"There are more than twice as many columns as the Parthenon. One hundred twenty-seven to be exact. Sixty-feet high. This was thought to be first temple made almost entirely of marble."

"It is an unbelievable piece of architecture. Didn't Alexander have something to do with the building of this?"

"No," Djinn said, a little forcefully. "Alexander tried. He arrived here in 333 B.C., while the temple was under construction, and offered to finance it if the people of Ephesus would give him credit as the builder. The city fathers did not want Alexander's name carved into the building, and one of the fathers shrewdly convinced him that one god should not build a temple for another god. Due to his enormous ego, Alexander agreed and left the city."

Gardner noticed the almost monotonous recital of information and Djinn's stoic face. "You were there," he stated.

Djinn said nothing.

"You hated him."

"He was my first owner."

"You don't want to talk about it?" Gardner didn't know why he was pressing Djinn. He had this need to know all about Djinn and what troubled him so.

"I have never spoken of it." Djinn paused. "But perhaps the time has come. At Pharos. I have never seen the Lighthouse. I swore never to return to Alexandria. I will break this promise for you."

Gardner couldn't respond. He turned from Djinn and walked into the Temple.

Djinn followed.

Gardner walked the long corridor of columns, seeing the statue of Artemis at the far end. A hand grasped his.

"I am sorry, Gardner. I do not mean to hurt you."

"I'm not hurt. But I know you're hurting every time I mention Alexander. I care about you and want to help you." Gardner felt that the next words he said would change his life forever. He stopped walking and looked at Djinn. "I love you."

Djinn's face was inscrutable. Gardner rushed on. "I know it's futile; it's all impossible, but I wanted you to know. Please don't say anything. I don't expect anything. How could I?"

Djinn's lips pressed to his.

The kiss continued and Djinn slowly lowered Gardner to the floor, never parting their lips.

Once again the cold marble was covered with soft cushioning. Fabric and feathers. The softest down enveloped them both. Their togas had vanished.

Djinn raised Gardner's arms and held them up. Djinn secured them with velvet cuffs and large linked chains. Gardner had no idea what they could have been connected to. He tugged. Bound. Hands and... feet. How? Magic, of course. Is this retribution for binding him up at the Tomb? Did I go too far? Does he hate me for telling him I love him? A long feather appeared in front of his face. It caressed his forehead and cheeks, tickled his nose his lips, sensitizing them. The feather was replaced by Djinn's own lips. The change from feather to flesh was startling and erotic. Djinn flicked his tongue over Gardner's lips, down to his chin, and up to his nose. He paused, saying, "Fire or ice?" He sat up, astride Gardner and held a lit candle in one hand and a very large cube if ice in the other.

Gardner stirred with excitement... and fear. He trusted Djinn. Didn't he? He'd asked Djinn to trust him. Was this Djinn doing the same? "Fire," he blurted.

"No more talking, Gardner." A silken gag, scented with... ambrosia filled Gardner's mouth. The heady scent and taste instantly recalled other acts of lovemaking.

Djinn raised the candle over Gardner's chest and turned it. Their eyes locked on the drip as it splashed onto Gardner's nipple.

A muffled "ahh" escaped from beneath the gag.

"Now ice." Djinn thrust the cube onto Gardner's newly waxed nipple.

Gardner bucked up into Djinn and gave another cry. The contrasting sensation incredible. He watched as Djinn moved to his other nipple. The anticipation was as powerful as the action. This time, knowing what was coming, heightened the feelings. Djinn coursed his way down Gardner's body, sides, inner thighs, ankles, insteps, toes. All the while Gardner anticipated the hot and cold and in the back of his mind, the ultimate sensations to his genitals.

Gardner was staring face down. He turned his head to side. He was still bound and gagged. As he reoriented himself, he felt the first drip of wax on his shoulder. It shocked him. Then the ice. Not being able to see now gave Djinn's actions a new perspective. He could only guess where the next drips would fall. "Mmph." His lower back. His buttocks, backs of thighs, knees, calves. The soles of his feet drew an almost violent movement from him. *I'm slowly dying... and I love it.*

Gardner was once more on his back. Djinn sat astride his thighs. His eyes blazed with heat and desire. He knew what was coming. Needed it. Djinn raised the candle and slowly dripped onto his testicles. Gardner bucked and writhed. Djinn remained firmly planted, as he brought the ice to bear.

Gardner pitched up violently again. *I know this will kill me. But if this how I'm going to die, I want it to be like this.*

Djinn repeated the process twice more. Each time bringing Gardner closer and closer to his climax.

Djinn dripped the wax once again, and as Gardner thrust up, Djinn took him in his mouth. Gardner was lost. With a final thrust upward, Djinn brought the ice down, only this time it went beneath his genitals and to the most sensitive spot between his buttocks.

Gardner screamed as he climaxed. And climaxed. It seemed it would never end, or that he would actually die from it.

He didn't die—which surprised him. How could a human being take so much? Time had passed, he didn't know how much. His breathing had slowed, and he began to become aware—aware that he was alive, aware that he was no longer bound or gagged, and aware that Djinn still had him in his mouth. He reached down and brought Djinn up to him. He looked at him and tried to decipher what he saw in his eyes. "Why?"

Djinn answered quietly, "I want you to trust me." Gardner noticed soft tears at the corners of his eyes.

"I do."

"Are you ready for the Lighthouse?"

"Are you?" Gardner couldn't help but saying.

"Yes. Now I am. Djinn took Gardner's hand."

Alexandria.

They stood on a long stone ramp, the Lighthouse before them, towering almost five hundred feet in the air. They were on the small island of Pharos, water everywhere. The city lay across the water in the distance.

"It is an impressive structure," Djinn said. "We are in 950 A.D., in case you were wondering. I chose this period because in a few years an earthquake will cause damage to the Lighthouse and the repairs will lower its height some seventy feet. You will be able to get photos of it in daylight, and when night falls in a couple of hours, you will be able to photograph it when the flames from the tower will be visible."

Gardner pulled Djinn to him and pressed his lips to Djinn's in a slow, deep kiss. "Thank you," he said after. "You seem to know exactly what I want," the double entendre intentional.

"I want you to be happy, Gardner."

Gardner turned away so that Djinn could not see the tears that sprang to his eyes. How can I be happy knowing all this will soon be over and I'll never see you again? He cleared his throat and changed the subject. "No more togas? And why do I have pants but no shirt?"

"I like you this way," Djinn said.

"Back at you, big guy." Gardner turned back to Djinn and gave a small caress of Djinn's chest before turning to his book. "It was built in three sections. The giant base two hundred and forty feet high sits on a twenty foot high platform." He looked up. "That seems about right."

"Would you like to measure it?" Djinn half laughed.

"That's all right. Maybe next time." Gardner's eyes misted again. *Except there will never be a next time. I need to keep it together and just enjoy our time together.* "It's also one hundred feet square. The second section is a one-hundred-and-fifteen-foot high, eight-sided tower. *Very cool. That had to be a pain to do.* Then the top is a sixty-foot-high cylinder with a cupola on top where the flame is, with the giant mirror to reflect the light. It says that the statue, way on top, is probably Poseidon." He stopped reading. "At least I'll get to confirm that, right?"

"Whatever you wish, Gardner."

"Are we still doing the 'wish' thing? There isn't anything I want to wish for." *What a whopper of a lie that is.*

"It is always in effect, Gardner."

"Ooookay." Gardner returned to his book once more. "Did you know that this was a tourist attraction? You can go up in the tower. And on the first level they sell food, for God's sake. Of course, I'm sure there are no vendors or other people there now." He gave a sidelong glance to Djinn in disapproval.

"An Egyptian religious feast today, I believe."

"Right. Let me get some shots." He photographed the tower as they proceeded up the ramp, Djinn silently watching him work, Gardner thinking all the while how great it would be or would have been to have Djinn with him wherever he went.

"I guess I don't need any shots from a different perspective as the tower is square," Gardner said, approaching a door in the structure. "We're pretty high up. There's nothing in the courtyard below us anyway. No food vendors or 'I climbed the Lighthouse at Pharos and all I got was this lousy T-shirt,' sellers."

"Did you want one?" Djinn asked.

Gardner thought a moment. "That might be fun. Let me think about it. There's supposed to be a spiral staircase through this door," he said, pointing in front of them.

The door opened by itself, revealing the staircase. "Must you?" Gardner said.

"I like to surprise you," Djinn said with a mischievous twinkle in his eye."

"I guess being here is not as traumatic as you'd thought?" Gardner hoped bringing up the giant elephant in the tower wasn't the wrong thing to do.

"It is because you are here with me. I am going to banish my former memories with memories of making love with you. I have something special in mind."

160

Gardner felt the heat rush through his body. "Everything is special with you, Djinn." He held Djinn's hand for a moment, then turned to mount the narrow staircase.

When they finally reached the top, the cupola stood before them, housing the light. The square viewing area around the cupola allowed them to walk around and view miles in the distance in every direction. "Wow. Once again, another magnificent view," Gardner said, looking out. Djinn came up behind him and encircled him with his arms. Gardner basked in the warmth of their upper naked bodies touching.

Gardner turned around in Djinn's arms and said, "But this is my favorite view." He stared into Djinn's eyes and brought his lips to Djinn's. The kiss was soft and sensuous. Their lips explored one another's, as if they were slowly melting together. The kiss deepened and their tongues continued the same exploration and melting. There was nothing frantic, only the pure enjoyment of what a kiss can be between two lovers.

Their hands followed a similar pattern as they discovered each other's backs and shoulders, slowly caressing, kneading, massaging—each touch purposeful. They eased down as one to the floor of the tower. Soft bedding provided by Djinn met their bodies. They spent many minutes indulging this way, both sensing a new connection between them, something stronger and deeper than before.

"Will you make love to me? No one has ever done that," Djinn whispered in Gardner's ear. "Nor have I ever wanted anyone to."

Gardner felt the earnestness and sadness in every fiber of his body. He knew Djinn had turned a corner with this revelation, only imagining what the years of being a slave to every kind of wanton desire could have entailed. He moved his mouth to Djinn's ear. "Yes. My love."

Djinn expelled a deep breath and pulled Gardner hard into his body. They hurriedly now removed each other's pants, never moving their mouths from one another, both needing the constant contact.

They explored each other, everywhere, almost as though it were the first time. Everything was new, every touch a mystery solved.

Gardner needed to pace himself, readying his mind and body to make it perfect for Djinn. He pulled his face back a moment from Djinn's. "Are you sure, Djinn? I want to please you."

"Gardner, I have never wanted anything more." Djinn's eyes held an intensity and desire that Gardner had not seen before. He wished Djinn loved him the way he loved Djinn. Maybe he does love me? He acts like it. But he hasn't said it. I only know I love him so much it physically hurts me. Oh Djinn, I want to be with you forever. That's the only wish I want you to grant me. As these thoughts whirled, he maneuvered himself between Djinn's legs, Djinn raising up and accommodating. "I love you," he said. His mouth met Djinn's and he joined them together.

Their lovemaking was beyond anything Gardner could have imagined. With Djinn's giving himself to him, Gardner's level of desire was intensified ten-fold.

As he reached the sought for climax, Gardner felt Djinn also peaking with him and manipulated himself toward his goal.

Djinn's threw his head back and cried out Gardner's name in an explosive release. Gardner, hearing his name fly from Djinn's lips and knowing he was the cause of the man's pleasure, thrust hard one last time to join in Djinn's bliss.

They lay locked together for several minutes, enjoying one another in silence while their breathing and heart rates returned to normal.

Djinn finally broke the silence. "I knew it would be perfect, Gardner."

Gardner rolled to his side to stare at Djinn. "I wanted it to be perfect for you." Then he hesitated a moment before saying, "Has it never been pleasurable for you?"

"It can only be pleasurable if it is with someone you care about. I have had degrees of satisfaction, but never pleasure." Djinn smiled softly. "You have shown me pleasure and much more."

Gardner's heart leapt. *Now I know he cares about me, even if he doesn't truly love me.* "Will you tell me about Alexander?"

Djinn's jaw clenched momentarily. "Yes. I believe I can talk about it with you. Alexander and Hephaestion. Never were a couple more suited. They were equally egocentric and cruel. They found the lamp while in Egypt on their conquering campaign, Alexander naming some seventeen cities Alexandria. Only this one still remains. Would that its name had also changed. I appeared to them much as I am now. I became an object of their sexual perversions and cruelty. They were very canny with their wishes. Alexander shared the lamp with Hephaestion, and in so doing guaranteed at least six wishes. Their wishes were all-encompassing and exacting. Wording was always precise, preventing misinterpretation." Djinn paused, composing his thoughts. "One of their wishes was that I would be their sex slave in perpetuity, allowing me no alternatives. I was continually beaten, raped by man and object and in every manner, knowing that I could not die but could certainly suffer. I was made to have sex with men, women, animals, and I had no recourse but to subjugate myself. Their limits on imagination knew no boundaries, and they were insatiable, especially after a battle. Their blood was high and only hours of seemingly endless sex would quench their fire. It was a blessing and a curse that I could heal myself, for no sooner would I then they would conceive some new torture."

Gardner was inwardly horrified. He took Djinn's hand and held it tight, knowing words were inadequate to the depredation Djinn had had to endure.

Djinn squeezed back, then continued, "I am very glad Alexander never saw the Lighthouse, for it is magnificent."

"That's right. This was built after he died," Gardner interjected. "How did you finally get away from those monsters?"

"It is against my code, if you will, for me to kill. I have no power over life and death. Alexander had left the city for a short while to oversee his territory. Hephaestion became gravely ill—poison, I suspect. For you see, they both had many enemies within their own camp who were not pleased with them. I was not the only recipient of their abuse. Mine was, perhaps, the most extreme, due to my immortal nature. We returned to the city after a messenger had informed Alexander of his lover's illness. Alexander, however, was not told of the gravity of the situation and so chose not to wish our swift return with my magic. It was to be his undoing. We arrived too late. Hephaestion had expired only hours before our return."

"That must have made you happy," Gardner said.

"Death is never happy, but I did feel relief and perhaps some justice. Alexander, though, became crazed. He ranted and raged, telling me to bring him back to life, which I could not. His grief drove him to make outrageous wishes, which now were not calculated. This gave me opportunity. In his subsequent campaigns throughout Asia Minor, his wishes became outrageous and never happened the way he envisioned them. He became incensed with me; his wishes became even more rage-filled and preposterous, until ultimately, he wished that I would go away. I was free of him, and he was killed shortly thereafter."

"Whoever could have known this, or suspected even?" Gardner said in disbelief. "There were others, too?"

"Yes, but none like they were. I could suffer the minor indignations of them. But they all followed the same pattern. The

165

more they received, be it power, riches, sex, the more they craved. These were not good people. They had the evil inside them, but by having me, they were able to expand upon it." Djinn had a resigned look on his face.

Gardner became afraid. *He thinks I'll become corrupt and betray him. And why wouldn't he? No one else has been good to him.* His heart broke for this man... and himself. *I need to make this right.* He squeezed Djinn's hand, trying to convey all the love he felt for him in this one gesture. "I think we should go back home now. I certainly have enough photos. I can't thank you enough... for everything." He wanted to grab onto Djinn and never let go. But he knew if he did, he would probably burst into tears.

Djinn had an odd look on his face, but only said, "If that is what you want."

They were back in the Cairo hotel room, everything appeared as it was before they'd left.

Gardner said, "Nothing's changed, has it? We've been gone for so long, yet you've returned us to the minute we left, didn't you?"

"Time is continuous," Djinn said as a matter of fact.

"Might I ask a favor?"

"What is it, Gardner?"

"Could you give me a few hours alone for me to write the text for the book? I need the quiet time to concentrate." He half-smiled. "You distract me."

"Of course."

Djinn disappeared.

Gardner broke down in tears.

Minutes later, there was a knock at the door. The door opened.

"I'm sorry, the door was open and I..." Petulia stared from the doorway. "Oh, my dear boy, what's wrong?" She rushed to the bed where Gardner lay huddled in a ball, sobbing.

"Tell me what's happened. Where's Djinn?"

Gardner cried harder.

Petulia held him in her voluminous embrace. "Get it all out, dear, then we'll talk."

Gardner cried and hugged her close, crying as if he would never stop.

After almost a half-hour, Gardner's heaving subsided, and he made a final sweep of tears from his face.

"That's better." Petulia brushed his hair back. "Now tell me everything."

And he did.

"And now I don't know what to do," Gardner almost shouted. "And I'm sure you think I'm insane!"

"Don't be foolish, dear boy," Petulia shook her head. "I knew something was up from when my pictures magically appeared. I've learned over the years never to deny what we don't know about. You do know that Djinn loves you?"

"I thought he might, but he's never said it." He felt the tears starting again. "And how can we have a future? He thinks I'll become corrupt, just like everyone else."

"Did he say that?"

"No, but his track record speaks for itself. Why would he think I'd be different?" Gardner wiped his cheeks again with another tissue that Petulia kept supplying.

"Because you are different, Gardner. I knew it the moment I met you in the pyramid, when I rudely bullied you into taking those pictures of me. Sometimes I'm so ashamed of myself. It's a defense mechanism I use. Otherwise who would pay attention to a fat old woman like me?"

"I think you're wonderful, Petulia." Gardner looked at her seriously. "I mean it. You'll find someone who'll discover that and appreciate it, too."

"Thank you. And that just confirms what I said about you. You're a good man." She patted his cheek. "Now what else?"

Well, he's immortal. Where do I go with that? I'll get all old and wrinkled... and he'll still be perfect."

"Gardner, he loves you. Not the exterior, the interior." Petulia touched his chest.

Gardner sat upright. "I have to let him go."

"What..."

"No, I have to free him—from the lamp. It's the only thing to do." Gardner nodded. "It's the right thing to do."

"Is that what you want?"

"It's what I want for him."

"What an extraordinary man you are. And if it is meant to be, it will. Remember that saying about, 'If you truly love someone, let them go, for if they come back, then they truly love you.'"

Gardner smiled. "I don't think that's quite right."

"I like my version better. Djinn is lucky to have known you." She patted his cheek once again.

"Ahem," came a voice from the chair in the corner behind them. "Am I interrupting? I got bored and couldn't stay away." Djinn shrugged his muscular shoulders.

"Oh, Djinn, so nice to see you again." Petulia smiled and stood. "I have to run. I know you boys have a lot to talk about. Maybe breakfast tomorrow, nine 'ish... if you're free?"

Gardner was silent. Free.

"We would love to, my dear lady," Djinn jumped in.

"Splendid. Good night." Petulia looked at Gardner. "Good luck."

"Thank you. Good night," Gardner said.

"Good luck?"

Gardner turned to Djinn. "Please come sit with me. I need to talk to you."

Djinn joined him on the bed. "What is it, Gardner?"

"I need to make another wish." Then Gardner thought. "Two wishes."

"Whatever you want."

"First wish. I want Petulia to find someone to love as she should be loved, someone to treasure her."

"Done," Djinn said. "I could not have made a better wish myself. She is a wonderful person." Djinn tried to take Gardner's hand, but he pulled away.

"Please don't... not now. I need to say this. And thank you for granting that wish for Petulia." Gardner held his hands together.

Djinn was silent.

"Now, I don't want you to deny this final wish or have you alter it to suit yourself. I need you to trust me on this."

"I trust you, Gardner."

Gardner looked in Djinn's eyes. "I believe you actually do. Thank you." He took a deep breath before speaking. "This has all been wonderful—no, beyond wonderful—perfect. I love you, you know that. But I also know it can't go anywhere. You're a djinn. You're immortal. I want to keep these memories forever locked in my mind, just as they are. I have the photos. It's enough." Well, that was a lie, but I need to protect myself. "I'll be fine."

"Gardner—"

"No. it's my decision. You promised to trust me. This is my wish." Gardner sucked in a breath. "I wish you to be a free man. Free of me and free of the lamp."

Djinn stared at him. A look of disbelief, amazement and... love? on his face. Then he disappeared.

Gardner stared at the empty space Djinn had just occupied, and wept.

The next morning, Gardner sat at the table set for four in the hotel's dining area, his face down, staring into his coffee cup.

"Yoohoo, Gardner!" Petulia called, approaching the table with an older, distinguished gentlemen, who reminded him of Anthony Hopkins. "I hope you don't mind, but I was out for a stroll earlier this morning. I couldn't sleep." She winked at Gardner. "And I bumped into Charles here, also out for a stroll. We started chatting and strolling... and here we are."

Gardner stood to take the man's proffered hand. "Very nice to meet you."

"You also, dear boy," Charles said. "This lovely woman, in her beautiful, flowered print, has bowled me over. She has told me quite a bit about you, and I look forward to your new book. I am an avid fan of the Ancient Wonders."

Gardner saw Petulia blush at the compliment. He liked him right away. He was perfect for Petulia. Thank you, Djinn, wherever you are. I hope you find happiness, too.

"Is everything all right, Gardner?" Petulia asked as she sat in the chair Charles had pulled out for her.

"Yes, I've settled everything here." He gave her a small smile.

Reaching across the table, Petulia took Gardner's hand and squeezed it in reassurance. "I know everything will work out right for you. I feel it in my heart. Everything is different today."

Gardner nodded, feeling his throat close. How can it work out right? The only 'right' would be if Djinn were here.

"I'm not late, am I?"

Three heads turned to see a tall, well-muscled, dark-haired man standing at their table.

Gardner held his breath. *It can't be. How?*

"Djinn!" Petulia squeaked. "You're timing couldn't better." She gave a knowing look to Gardner. "This is my new friend, Charles."

"A pleasure." Djinn shook the man's hand and sat next to Gardner. "I feel that this is going to be a very special day for all of us." He looked at Gardner. "I see everything in a new light. I feel as if a huge weight has been lifted from my shoulders. A freedom. It's almost magical." He took Gardner's hand.

"Magical," Gardner echoed. *I know this can't be real. I freed him. Maybe I didn't. Maybe he can't be freed. I need to put up a good front here and make nice. I'm just happy he's here. I'll enjoy it and question later.*

They ate and talked as if they'd all been friends for years, Gardner joining in enthusiastically, trying not to figure out how or why this was all possible.

Finally, Petulia said, dabbing at her mouth, "We'll let you boys be alone for now. I can't eat another bite. It seems I don't want to eat as much as I usually do. I guess that's a good thing." She laughed. "I hope we'll see each other later."

"We will," Djinn assured. "Nice to meet you, Charles. Take good care of our Petulia. She's very precious to us."

"I intend to, Djinn. I can see she's very special," Charles said. He took Petulia's hand.

"I really like him. I think he'll be good for her," Gardner said, watching the older couple walk away, Petulia giving a last wave over her shoulder. "Thank you."

"It was my pleasure, Gardner." Djinn stared into his eyes. "I believe you have some questions?"

Gardner nodded.

"Let's go up to the room."

They sat on the bed, not touching, Gardner faced Djinn and said, "It didn't work, did it?"

"Of course it did. You wished it."

"But you haven't changed. You look the same."

"Gardner, this has always been my appearance. Others have chosen to see me differently. Only you, with your pure, unselfish heart could see the true person."

Gardner felt humbled. "Are you human, then? Are you mortal?"

"As far as I know. Time will tell." Djinn grinned.

Gardner took a breath before saying, "Are you here to stay?"

"Only on one condition."

I knew it. Gardner didn't want to ask. "What condition?"

"That you wish... me to stay."

Djinn's look was so tender, it almost broke Gardner's heart. "I wish it more than anything I've ever, or could ever, want." Gardner threw his arms around Djinn. "I love you so much." His voice broke. "I can't live without you." He felt the tears coming to his eyes.

Djinn's mouth found his ear, and said, "I cannot live without you either, Gardner. You've shown me what it is to love... and more importantly, to be loved—truly—for who I am as a man."

Gardner pulled back to see Djinn face. "Then... you love me?"

"I believe I loved you from the moment you said it would be a pleasure to have 'our lovely little Petulia' join us for dinner. I saw the man you were then. It was such a touching, kind, selfless gesture." Djinn put his hand on Gardner's cheek. "Yes, Gardner, I love you. And I only hope to be half the man that you are."

"Djinn, you're more than I ever could have wished for. Nothing could ever be more magical." Gardner frowned. "Your magic is gone, then? I'm sorry about that."

"Gardner, the magic is you." Djinn leaned in with a kiss so tender and loving that Gardner could have died on the spot and been happy.

When they broke, Djinn said, "Have you thought about your next book? I can be of use, you know. I have traveled many places."

"I may try some other ancient ruins: Machu Picchu, Stonehenge, the Nazca lines."

"I have some knowledge." Djinn gave a mysterious smile.

"I can't wait." Gardner now took his turn and touched Djinn's cheek. "And can we make love at all those places, too?"

"That was my plan." Djinn pulled his face close to Gardner's and whispered. "We have several hours until dinner. I would love to make love with you until then."

Gardner sucked in a breath and wet his lips. "I would like that, too."

"Where would you like to go?"

Gardner looked at him puzzled. "Here is fine, or anywhere. I only know that I wish to be with you." He ran his hand down Djinn's chest and between his legs. "Surprise me."

Djinn's hand met Gardner's at the juncture between his legs. "Close your eyes."

Gardner did so, waiting for Djinn's lips to meet his. They didn't. Gardner opened his eyes.

Machu Pichu.

ABOUT THE AUTHOR

Lance Taubold is the recipient of the IBPA Ben Franklin Award for BEST FIRST NON-FICTION for ON TWO FRONTS. He has been an entertainer for 25 years, performing at the MET Opera, on Broadway and on television for 5 years on the soap opera "General Hospital." As a writer he has written for Envy Man magazine, both as a fiction writer and book reviewer. His first novel RIPPER A LOVE STORY was written with author Richard Devin.

Taubold is the author of the gay, paranormal romance series: ZODIAC LOVERS BOOKS 1-5.

Taubold has been a contributor to all of the award-winning NEVER FEAR horror anthologies, the UNCHARTED WORLDS-XENO ENCOUNTERS sci-fi anthology and has romance stories in ROMANTIC TIMES: VEGAS, and THE HAUNTED WEST. His next release is the gay romance, murder mystery MAGIC, MURDER AND MISTLETOE. He is currently writing a paranormal romance series with New York Times Bestselling author Heather Graham.

INVOKE BOOKS

Adventures in all Genres

Exciting Thrillers, Heart-Warming Romance,
Mind-Bending Horror, Sci-Fantasy
and
Educational Non-Fiction

InvokeBooks.com

facebook.com/InvokeBooksPublisher

Feed an Author...

Leave a Review

Never Fear Series

New York Times bestselling authors, Heather Graham, F. Paul Wilson, Jon Land, Michael Stackpole, Matthew Costello, William F. Nolan and award-winning, master story tellers bring the best in tales of horror.

Never Fear
Shh… Something's Coming…

Never Fear – Phobias
Everyone Fears Something

Never Fear - Christmas Terrors
He Sees You When You're Sleeping…

Never Fear - The Tarot
Do You Really Want To Know…

Never Fear – Apocalypse
The End is Near…

RT Booklovers Presents: The Haunted West

Written especially for RT Booklovers, best-selling and award-winning authors Diana Gabaldon, Heather Graham, Virginia Henley, Kat Martin, Katherine Neville, Bobbi Smith, Tina Wainscott, Tina DeSalvo and more... take you on a time-traveling, spellbinding journey through America's sprawling West.

The Haunted West, Volume 1

The Haunted West, Volume 2

Romantic Times: Vegas

The Excelsior Hotel and Casino.in Las Vegas is the setting of these magical stories of romance. For decades the towering hotel has been the subject of incredible stories and rumors. Bestselling authors, Christina Skye, Heather Graham, Tina DeSalvo and a story by the Lady of Barrow, Kathryn Falk will take you deep into the heart of those, in the past, present and future... who roam the halls of the Excelsior in search of that perfect love.

Volume 1

Volume 2

Volume 3

Heather Graham's Christmas Treasures

Heather Graham's Haunted Treasures

Presented together for the first time, New York Times Bestselling Author, Heather Graham brings back three out-of-print Christmas classics that are sure to inspire, amaze, and warm your heart.

Heather Graham's Christmas Treasures also available in **Invoke Books Dyslexic Friendly**

New York Times Bestselling Author, Heather Graham brings back three tales of paranormal love and adventure.

The Third Hour

Winner of the USA Best Book Award - Thrillers

The Third Hour is an original spin on the religious-thriller genre, incorporating elements of science fiction along with the religious angle. Its strength lies in this originality, combined with an interesting take on real historical figures, who are made a part of the experiment at the heart of the novel.

Ripper – A Love Story

Prince Edward Albert Victor, The Duke of Clarence is Queen Victoria's favorite grandson and the most eligible bachelor in England. Coren Butler has captured his heart in the perfect Cinderella story. A dream come true. Then the nightmare begins.

Uncharted Worlds: Xeno Encounters

Uncharted Worlds—an exciting new speculative fiction series featuring bestselling and award-winning authors. Ten mind-boggling adventures include tales of ancient aliens, other worlds, and imagined futures.

On Two Fronts

IBPA Silver Medal Best Non-Fiction Award Winner

When two unlikely friends are separated by war, they must learn to cope with the effect it will have on their lives, their futures, and their relationship.

Bad Attitude/Diamond in the Rough

Bad Attitude Meet bad boy, undercover state trooper Reid Cameron. Meet Polly Sweet, the woman who is about to be his downfall. In order to catch a jewel thief, Cameron wants to use Polly's house, and he comes up with a plan, whereby they play at being lovers. But when the first play-acted kiss happens, neither one is ready for the feelings that kiss ignites or for the consequences that ensue.

Has this bad boy finally met his match? How Bad is Too Bad?

Diamond In The Rough-Detective Dan Murdock is on a dangerous stakeout, when advice columnist, Millie Gordon unwittingly shows up on the scene, putting them both in danger. To save her from possibly being shot when the mobsters arrive, Murdock jumps into Millie's car and throws himself over her to protect her, little realizing that the real danger starts when their bodies come together.

Romance and action are the name of the game in this two-in-one duo from bestselling author Doris Parmett

Calendar Girl

Fate, it seems, has derailed destiny… and found a love for all time. Tina Wainscott weaves a tale you'll not soon forget.

Family

Matthew Costello's widely acclaimed post-apocalyptic thriller, comes to it's amazing conclusion.

Treasures and Pleasures

A Collection of Romantic Novellas from the bestselling author Bobbi Smith.

Shadows in the Big Easy

Bouchercon Presents stories by up and coming Teen Writing Contest winners in this mystery anthology.

Stop Saying Yes – Negotiate!

Stop Saying Yes - Negotiate! is the perfect "on the go" guide for all negotiations. Fortune 500 Companies world-wide send out their teams of negotiators with copies tucked away in briefcases and notebooks... maybe you should too?

Do You Want To Be An Actor?

101 Answers To Your Questions About Breaking Into The Biz from people who know, Casting Directors, Producers, Directors and Agents tell it like it is.

Zodiac Lovers Series

In this series of romantic, gay, paranormal stories tales of love lost, love found, and love to last for eternity will fill your heart with awe and your eyes with tears.

Zodiac Lovers 1: Aquarius, Pisces, Aries

Zodiac Lovers 2: Taurus, Gemini, Cancer

Zodiac Lovers 3: Leo, Virgo, Libra

Zodiac Lovers 4: Scorpio, Sagittarius, Capricorn

Zodiac Lovers 5: Cetus, Ophiuchus

www.ingramcontent.com/pod-product-compliance
Lightning Source LLC
Chambersburg PA
CBHW070852120626
46556CB00002B/953